Patrick stroked his hand delicately through her hair. The feel of her hair gave him great pleasure. The silky fibers slipping through his fingers were so sensual. His eyes fixed on hers, "Your last chance, my pet, from this point on you will be my possession to do with as I see fit. Do you submit?"

Patrick looked into her eyes and saw his intensity mirrored in her eyes.

She smiled and replied, "With all my heart, I submit to you."

Her words flowed over him like a summer breeze on a hot day. Her gift to him was more precious than anything in the world. His heart lifted to new heights as the intoxicating power she bestowed on him surged through him. He bristled with excitement the hairs on the back of his neck standing as erect as his penis. He was so proud of her, ecstatically empowered by the trust she gave him so freely.

He looked deeply into her pale green eyes, "What we will do here today will be for our mutual pleasure."

The smile and slow deliberate nod was her reply.

"Very well my pet." The merest touch to her head indicated he wanted her to kneel and without hesitation, she complied.

www.blackvelvetseductions.com

Ric Savage weaves together a fantastic tale of power exchange and romance where the lovers are living out their dreams on borrowed time. I am truly delighted by the story and look forward to more by this author.

Robert Cloud – Author
Toy's Story: Acquisition of a Sex Toy & The Crimson Z

Ric Savage has once again touched the heart of this reader. His first published work in "The Crimson Z" brought tears to my eyes and these two works brought smiles to my lips. The relationship between the Dominant and submissive is explained very well in "Temporally Yours" and if you ever had any questions about those relationships, Ric has answered them here.

Lee Rush – Author
Bound by Fate & The Crimson Z

www.blackvelvetseductions.com

Richard Savage

Temporally Yours
&
The Key

Thank You so much, enjoy the read

Ric

ISBN 0-9802246-1-6

Copyright 2008 Richard Savage
Cover Art Copyright 2008 by Richard Savage
www.swage.net

All rights reserved. No part of this book may be used or reproduced in any manner whatsoever without written permission, except in the case of brief quotations embodied in critical articles or reviews.

All characters in this book are completely fictional. They exist only in the imagination of the author. Any similarity to any actual person or persons, living or dead, is completely coincidental.

Published 2008
Printed by Black Velvet Seductions Publishing Company in the United States of America

Visit us at:
www.blackvelvetseductions.com

Acknowledgments

This book is a result of many years spent as an artist, looking at and working with people who live alternative lifestyles. In that time I have seen most things and I have to say that my view of what normal is, is probably a bit broader than some people's. The ideas in this book are fictional, yet there are little details that have been carefully borrowed from people I have known, and for whom I have great respect.

This book was written with the help and support of my friend, editor and publisher Laurie Sanders, without whose support and belief in me as a writer, this story would be on a dusty hard drive never to see the light of day. I would also like to thank the Black velvet Seductions family of artists and writers who have also given me their support and help.

Last, and by no means least, I would like to thank my long suffering wife, who puts up with my creative untidiness and without who's unwavering support, I would never have been able to follow my artistic dreams.

Temporally Yours

Chapter One

Time on my Hands

The air was filled with the pungent aroma of coffee and Danish pastries. Smells of cooking wafted from the kitchen. Waitresses bustled, taking and delivering orders and there was a general buzz in the background as people discussed the minutia of their daily lives.

Patrick closed the case of his gold pocket watch with a satisfying click. 11:37 AM. He stroked the inlayed and engraved watchcase, enjoying the tactile feel, before slipping it into his vest pocket. Absorbed, Patrick was oblivious to the room's distractions.

He sat, warming his hands on the mug, staring into his coffee noir, contemplating time, seeing the world over the cup's white rim. Time was the thing, there was never enough of it, or at least that used to be the case.

To be in control of time, was to be the master of your own destiny. All those wasted hours, ticking away, gone forever, like grains of sand lost on a beach. But what if you could stop time and live in the gaps, he wondered.

It was a fantasy for a man waiting. Time. If he had a wish, it would be to spend more time with Susan. He was haunted by a reoccurring daydream of Susan being a part of his every day life.

A noise distracted him and for a moment, he looked around the café. His eyes were drawn to the source of the noise, a red-faced waitress, frantically apologizing to customers, amidst a pile of mangled food and broken crockery. The room was caught up in the drama for a moment, and then it returned to its low rumble of chatter. For a moment, he listened to the overlapping waves of conversation. Other people's lives had always fascinated him.

There was something of the voyeur in him, picking at the threads as people chatted, in the vague hope of a juicy tid-bit. Although years had ticked by the topics of the conversation had not changed, who was sleeping with whom, the price of food, and the scandalous behavior of whatever administration was currently in the White House. The Café itself was timeless. It still had all the hallmarks of the 1980's. Patrick had first sat here when it was new and besides looking a little tatty, nothing much had changed. He found he liked the continuity.

His finger idly played with some spilled sugar on the table and the individual snippets of conversation returned to a background drone, freeing his mind to drift back to his coffee and time.

He remembered books he had read and films he had seen. There was a scene from a science fiction film regarding the nature of time, and a conversation, his mind struggled to recall.

"They say time is a beast that stalks us all our lives," Dr. Soren had said in the film.

"I prefer to think of time as a friend that accompanies us along our journey" Picard had responded.

He had sat on both sides of that fence. For so many years of his life, he had thought of time as the enemy and now time was just a thing that was there. It was just a factor, like the weather, always there. No longer the demon it once was.

He took the watch from his pocket, the gold chain dangled

from the round ring on the winding stem. Patrick pressed the knurled winding button and the case sprung open 11:59 AM. His heart raced as the bell on the café door rang. He looked up from the watch as Susan entered.

He closed the watch and returned it to its pocket. He could see her eyes searching for him and he caught her gaze. They both smiled. The connection made, they didn't break eye contact as he rose to greet her.

She looked smart, yet he could see she had come straight from work, by the wrinkle lines in her dark skirt. There was that worn all day look about her clothes, but they were smart nonetheless.

He had missed her and joy filled his heart, as she picked her way to his table. He moved into the gap between the closely spaced tables, trying to avoid the clutter of handbags and general shopping debris, and held his arms out to greet her. He could see his smile mirrored on her face as they melted into each other's arms.

He loved the feel of her soft lips as they grazed lightly against his. Her lips parted slightly, surrendering to the tip of his penetrating tongue. He was aware of his penis stirring, like some caged animal, in its dark confined space. He suspected too that people were beginning to notice them.

The kiss deepened and he ran his hand across Susan's pert bottom, and gave her tender cheek a squeeze. He wanted her here and now, yet for the sake of decency he knew he would have to break soon.

Still locked in a hug, Patrick reluctantly broke the kiss. It had lasted a matter of seconds but it had felt a lifetime. Slowly he became aware that the chatter had stopped and to his amusement he discovered that they were indeed, attracting a substantial amount of attention from the cafés other occupants.

With a last squeeze of her ass, he smiled and said, "God I have missed you." He kissed her again, holding her against him. Though it had been only days, it felt an age since they had been together.

He lingered with the kiss letting his lips slip to her slender neck, as he drank in her floral fragrance. She always smelled good even after a day at work. He felt her hair on his cheek. It was long and loose, soft and shiny, falling in soft shimmering waves that framed her face. He could not help himself, his hand rose to feel the silken strands, fine as gossamer. His nose touched her hair and his nostrils detected a little of the hair spray, that had recently been combed out.

Usually when they met, with Susan coming straight from work, her hair was still in the airline regulation tight bun. It gave him pleasure to see her hair let loose. The hazel colored tresses curled under slightly giving it a gentle bounce, when she moved.

His eyes wandered down her length. Each time they met it took his breath away how beautiful she was and how lucky he was to call her his. He loved the way she looked in her uniform, strangely sexy. The smartly tailored dark blue jacket molded to the line of her breast and the matching skirt clung pleasingly to her hips. Both bore little creases, showing all the signs of a hard day's work and that too was erotic, the lines of the distressed fabric, showing her body's movement. He found it a huge turn on that she had come straight from work. Her urgency to see him echoed his and made him stiffen. His erection was beginning to make its own demands. Her smile was pure lust. The glint in her eye, as she looked deeply into his gaze told him of the passion that burnt within her and the flush on her cheek and neck showed him, beyond doubt, that she was as needy as he was.

In his mind's eye he pictured her naked, in his arms, as they lay together on a bed with crisp white sheets, basking in the afterglow of their spent passion. His erection moved uncomfortably. He struggled with the urge to straighten it, but this was far too public a place. He squeezed her bottom.

A clatter of cutlery and the slowing chatter of the other

diners sank into Patrick's consciousness, reminding him of how public they still were. In truth he was so focused on Susan he didn't really give a shit how public they were, his need to have her clouded everything else.

Susan smiled and said, "I have been counting down the seconds." She beamed and reciprocated his action, her fingers feeling his buttocks beneath the soft material of his suit pants. She stroked the rounded contour of his bottom. She loved the feel of his tight muscular ass. She felt herself moisten, in anticipation of the fun and games that were yet to come.

She tightened her grip. "I thought I would never get here, it has taken forever." She could tell by the look on his face and the bulge pressing against her, that he was as hungry as she was. "The taxi took forever to get here."

Susan looked deeply into his warm hazel eyes, kissed him and whispered into his lips, "It is wonderful to see you, I have missed you so much." She pulled him closer and kissed him, inhaling his subtle spicy aromatic aftershave. She loved that scent, loved the way the smell of him lingered on her clothes. The smell of him never failed to make her knees weaken and her panties moisten.

She was very aware of the closeness of his body; the feel of his erection pressed to her was unmistakable. The way he pulled her tightly to him, left her in no doubt of the depth of his desire for her. The flush on her cheek and the ache in her breast made her burn for time alone with the man she knew was the only man in the world for her. The hunger she felt consumed her waking thoughts and prowled her dreams.

They reluctantly broke apart. Patrick characteristically pulled out the chair for her, and caught the waitress's eye with an equally polite, "Please."

She had been drawn to Patrick from the first time they had flown on the same plane. He had been a regular passenger when she worked on the Washington to California route.

There had been something magnetic about his personality. An understated power, the way he held himself, so upright so self-assured, that had attracted her to him.

He dressed immaculately; he had always worn a three-piece black suit and had always looked fresh when he'd flown her route. She'd found herself hovering near his seat, waiting for him to press the attendant button and had been a little despondent when he didn't call. When on the rare occasion he did call there was always a spring in her step. It was instinctual, she had felt from the start that she wanted to be with him, wanted to serve him.

She'd kept looking for signs that he was spoken for, a wedding band, something to shatter her illusion, but she never saw any evidence of a woman in his life.

He was good looking, but she was impressed as much by his manners which were impeccable, always a please and thank you. Always a pleasant smile.

Over the weeks, she had found herself leading up to starting her first non-airline conversation with him. She had felt like she was back at school, with all the little girl butterflies, but she had started the conversation.

It had happened when they had been on a late flight to Washington, on a Wednesday night. The plane was almost empty. She knew his name from the flight manifest, and she had been plucking up the courage to chat with him. "Mr. Ryan, is there anything I can do to make your flight more pleasant?" she had asked.

Their eyes had met and he had smiled. "I am fine thank you, but if you are free, it would be nice to talk. It has been a long day and a little company would be nice."

She smiled, relieved that he had helped to break the ice. They chatted on and off for the rest of the flight, about everything and nothing. From that conversation, their relationship grew.

They had chatted on other flights, and after awhile had swapped phone numbers and shared meals when they were in the same city. Eventually they shared nights together when they were in the same city.

From the very beginning, she had wondered what it would be like to be with him, what it would be like to he held in his strong arms. She had more than once found herself moistening thinking of those passionate moments. When working away, she spent many nights in lonely hotel rooms. As she laid beneath crisp, white, Egyptian cotton sheets, it was the thoughts of Patrick that lit her fire. It was thoughts of his hands roaming freely over her body, opening her, possessing her, that took her to the edge, while her fingers deftly strummed her sweet pearl of pleasure.

It was those thoughts of Patrick that fuelled her fantasies. Deep dark fantasies, of her tied, while he ravished her defenseless body. Happy sun light fantasies of making love on a warm summer's afternoon. Regardless of scenario, it was always Patrick, her own personal knight in shining armor that protected her and kept her from harm. It was thoughts of Patrick's hands on her that fuelled her when her fingers traveled south. As fantasy and physical peaks came together, Patrick took her over the edge.

Her mind played through the fantasies and feelings of being possessed and taken. The dawn of reality brought her back to Patrick's physical presence, across from her in the café. She loved the feel of his warm palm lightly touching hers as they sat holding hands, their conversation a light soufflé of well-humored chat, as they caught up with each other's lives.

Her work schedule had changed, creating a longer gap between the times they were together. It had been just two weeks to the day since they had last met, but that two weeks had felt like an eternity. She had hungered for each stolen moment, each phone call, text message, e-mail, anything. She had felt lost and without direction while they were apart.

She had found that she needed him more and more and although the separation made her ache for him, there was a comfort in that ache, because it carried with it, the knowledge that he was right for her. She squeezed his hand and was delighted to feel him give a gentle squeeze back.

Patrick was delighted to have his lady back by his side. The time apart had taken its toll on him. He had found himself listless at meetings and distracted when he should have been focused. He had found himself fighting the urge to phone at inappropriate times. He had taken to restricting their calls to evenings, but oh such passionate evenings. He'd been amazed at the levels of passion that could be achieved through a simple phone line.

It was masturbation, yes, but it was different when two minds were linked in the act. They had explored the sensual world, their thoughts and suggestions escalating their passion. They'd explored themes from bondage and submission, to wispy light quests into the erotic.

It had been as if their two freethinking, willing minds had locked together as one in a kaleidoscope of erotic imagery. He felt himself stiffen further as he recalled their phone calls, but he hoped his hunger did not spill out in his conversation as he asked, "Have the flights been ok?" He felt her squeeze his hand.

Susan heard his words, but the look in his eyes said I want you now! She loved to see him this hungry, it made her feel wanted, desired. She knew he would engage in this polite discourse and she loved him for it, but she also knew him well enough to know the smoldering desire that lay below the controlled exterior.

Her tongue flicked out to moisten her lips and she heard herself say, "The flights were good, mostly on time," when what she wanted to say was, I am yours for the taking.

He smiled and squeezed her hand, letting his fingers stroke the palm of her hand "That is good, it is a chore when there are delays."

She had always thought he would make a good actor, as at a glance he appeared cool and relaxed, but her well-trained eye could see the trace of perspiration on his brow, his fingertips fiddled idly with his cufflinks. She loved that twitchy look he had about him, he was like a coiled spring, a cobra about to strike, and she liked him edgy like this.

Her clit tingled and her panties dampened. She felt so desired and this fuelled her own passion. God she wanted him and wanted him now. She wanted him so badly she ached. Her nipples felt caged within the confines of her bra, she wanted the bulge that she knew was straining to get out of Patrick's pants, buried deep inside her. The tease and denial of their public circumstances, was driving her to distraction. She ached for release. If only she could touch her clit, she knew she would cum on the spot.

She had to get her mind off her carnal desires or she would go crazy from the persistent throb between her legs. She desperately tried to think of something innocuous to say, "How about you? How has your work been?" she asked. She desperately wanted to sound interested, and she was interested, yet her own body's call distracted her. She squeezed her legs together in an attempt to quiet the throb within her, but that only served to stimulate her more. "I know you said it was not going smoothly."

Her bottom moved on the chair. She longed to quell the ache between her legs. It would take the merest touch to bring her to climax.

"Did you get the new database up and running eventually? You said you were having problems?" She smiled and stroked his hand. She loved his big strong hands. He could have been a construction worker with hands like that, so big, so powerful, yet soft, smooth and manicured. She longed to feel his hands on her body and craved the moment when he would possess her.

He loved the soft feel of her warm hand stroking his. She was so gentle. He looked into her eyes as he said, "We launched it yesterday, seems to be working well." His words came as if from another, for his mind was in a different place. The tender feel of her touch took his mind to more earthy places. He felt his penis throb, as he pictured her naked. He cupped his other hand over hers capturing it. His mind took him to tender thoughts of dungeons and chains where his pet would be oh so sweetly punished.

She loved the caged, captured, helpless feeling of his hands confining hers. She moistened, and a myriad of snippets of fantasies dashed through her mind. The slave girl imprisoned in a harem, at her master Patrick's beck and call, to be used and lovingly abused. The helpless maiden locked up high in an ivory tower, her jailer, Patrick a ruthless potentate. The humble housemaid on her knees serving her master Patrick, or whatever master he saw fit to give her to.

Patrick's hand was warm and firm, holding her. His hand made her feel so secure. He was the man who caged her heart and soul, and she would give her soul so eagerly.

She felt his weight, as he leaned in conspiratorially and whispered in her ear "Are you wearing them?" She smiled and felt the rush of heat that she knew must be coloring her cheeks. She looked at Patrick. He smiled warmly and squeezed her hand. Susan knew she could not hide her embarrassment. She sat mute, for a moment.

She put a finger to her lips and with a simple shush tried to quiet him.

She saw him raise his eyebrows, which she read as him telepathically re-asking the same question.

There was a jug of ice water on the table, she reached out and rested her free hand on the cold condensation on the glass. She felt the stark contrast between the iced jug and the heat of her face. Taking her hand from the water jug she placed it on her face, the affect was soothing. As she felt the flush in her cheeks subside, she began to see the funny side and the feeling of amusement grew. The fact that he should be so playful, as to even whisper this in a public place was kind of funny.

She began to look around, suddenly concerned. Had

anyone heard? She let out a nervous laugh, coughed to compose herself.

She paused and answered, "Yes. Of course I am wearing them." She felt herself flush again. Her free hand touched the jug of ice water again. She lifted the wonderfully chilled carafe off the table and brought it to her face.

Patrick beamed like a schoolboy. "Excellent, I hoped you would. I am so pleased" He squeezed her hand and asked excitedly, "How do they fit?"

She squeezed his hand back and beckoned with a finger to her lips for him to lower his voice. In hushed tones of her own, she said, "Like a glove." The intimacy of this conversation made her a little uncomfortable, yet excited. She moved in her seat, aware of the tightness in her body, the ache of her hardening nipples, nipples that felt caged as they rubbed against her bra. She felt an instant throb from between her legs, a pulse, emanating from that tiny hooded pearl and a deep intense hunger. Moistness spread from deep within. She wanted him. Now.

His hands held hers and he whispered, "When did you put them on?" She knew that he wanted to know everything, and her excitement had moved her beyond the point of caring, if they were being overheard or not. Was he as turned on as she was?

She tensed her muscles and was very aware of what she was wearing. Still feeling a little flushed, she snatched a glance around to see if anyone was actually eavesdropping. She was relieved to find they didn't seem to be. The people around, were all caught up in their own conversations. "Well, I couldn't fly wearing them."

"No, of course not." He paused, leaned across, kissed her cheek, and with a disarming smile spread over his lips said, "But, when?"

She could not help loving his enthusiasm, and the fact he was so energized made her hunger even stronger. The naughtiness of being so public was a big turn on too, yet what she wanted was privacy. She wanted his hand, his mouth, his cock, to sate her lust and the fact they were so exposed made for an exquisite game of tease and denial. She squirmed in her seat and felt her wetness grow.

She wanted so much to please him, to tell him all he wanted to hear. The desire to please was an ache deep within her, an ache she needed to rub. Her mind drifted back to the previous night in her lonely hotel room and the sound of his voice telling her what a good girl she was. She loved the praise, craved his approval. She would gladly give him anything, her body, her soul.

She was aware that she had fallen silent, lost in her daydream. She saw him raise a quizzical eyebrow as he was waiting patiently for her answer. Again, she composed her concentration enough to talk. "In the ladies room just before I got the taxi." She smiled, again trying to conceal her embarrassment, yet feeling herself blush a deeper pink. This public discussion was exciting, yet she yearned to take this conversation to a private place. Still she knew it was Patrick's desire to keep this part public. She knew he was enjoying her discomfort and she enjoyed giving him anything he wanted. This public conversation was just one way she would serve him.

She felt a profound urge to serve him, to give him everything he wanted. The way he gave her time, never rushing her, always taking her needs into consideration made her feel loved, nurtured, cherished. She loved Patrick, her master, and she wanted to give him everything, her body, her soul, everything.

Patrick could see desire smoldering in her eyes. He recognized it easily, as looking into her eyes, he saw the reflection of his own lust. He loved the way she looked slightly uncomfortable talking about such private matters in such a public place. He took great pleasure from the fact that he was putting her in a slightly uncomfortable position, taking her outside her comfort zone. He was also hugely turned on by the fact that she had risen to the challenge.

"How do they feel to wear?" His curiosity knew no bounds, but he sensed her discomfort with such an open conversation, even if he had whispered the question. The power it gave him thrilled him. His groin ached. His penis yearned to be set free. He leaned in a little closer to hear her whispered reply.

"They feel *very* different. Nice, but different."

He slipped his hand from hers and let it glide beneath the table letting it rest on her thigh. Susan squeezed his hand between her warm thighs and he knew it would not be long before they would have to leave.

"I can't wait to see, I bet they look phenomenal on you." He squeezed her thigh again feeling hot flesh beneath sheer nylon. He leaned in and kissed her on the cheek.

Patrick raised his hand to attract the waitress and indicated he wanted her attention. As she came to the table he said, "May I have the check please?"

The girl produced a slip of paper and Patrick fished a bill large enough to cover the check with a handsome tip from his wallet and told the waitress she could keep the change. She smiled, thanked him and moved away into the noise of other patrons.

"I have a hotel room booked across the block," Patrick said with another squeeze of Susan's hot skin.

"Tonight you will serve me totally," he whispered. He pictured in his mind's eye a myriad of service that echoed his heart's desire. There were scenes of loving bondage, tender discipline and scenes of her sweet surrender. These lust-filled thoughts, took his need, his hunger to new heights. He felt the ache of his groin as each moment took him closer to being alone with his love. With each second that ticked by the caged animal became more agitated, straining to be loosed from his pants. A bead of perspiration trickled down his cheek. He thought of the wetness between her legs and how he wanted to dive into her hot moist centre, gorge himself, devour her, take her, with his mouth then with his cock.

Chapter Two

Time and Tide

The business in the café completed, Patrick picked up his briefcase and taking her hand, ushered Susan, through the maze of crowded tables, to the exit.

His heart was filled with joy as hand in hand, they walked down the street.

He loved the happy metallic clatter of her heels on the pavement; it was the sound of his dreams coming to fruition. The air was hot and muggy, the smell of car exhausts, the waft of scents, the perfume of a fellow pedestrian, the smell of fresh bread from a patisserie, and the aroma of rich dark coffee from a street café, were all woven into a rich tapestry for the senses. The street was filled with the metropolis' hubbub and the pavement bustled with shoppers. As they walked to the hotel, they were pushed closer together. Patrick slipped his arm across her shoulders and guided her through the jostling people.

In Patrick's eyes, Susan appeared small and defenseless. Protectiveness swelled within him as they moved along the street. It was a wonderfully empowering feeling, to be the one in control, and the responsibility sat comfortably on his shoulders.

It was breathtaking to be that needed. He craved her need. More than raw animal desire, though in truth it was that too, he loved her with all his heart. He wanted Susan by his side every day, not just for these wonderful, passionate, trysts. He felt so alive and he wanted to feel this way, be this close to Susan every day, for the rest of his life.

His pace quickened. He wanted to get her alone as soon as he could.

With his arm tight around her, Susan felt safe. So close to this large protective man, she felt that nothing could harm her.

She looked up at him as they walked towards the hotel. Their eyes met, that smoldering look of desire told her all she needed to know. He was strong and steady as a rock. She saw in his warm, hazel eyes openness and honesty. She knew he would never hurt her and for all these reasons, she trusted him completely. Her heart was full of joy. She could not wait to be possessed by her Lord and Master.

As Patrick checked in Susan stood a pace or so behind. It was a busy place, all the better for this tryst, nobody would know or care about their presence. The hotel foyer was much the same as she had seen on her stopovers, a little ostentatiously decorated and looking as if a coat of paint would not go amiss. Low maintenance rented potted palms were scattered in interesting nooks in the wall. People mulled waiting for bellhops. She was vaguely aware of the conversation Patrick was having with the receptionist. He seemed delighted, when he came back to her.

"I have the key sweetie. I have asked for a nice quiet room." He smiled conspiratorially. "I have specifically asked for a secluded place, where we won't be seen.

Susan returned his smile and said cheekily, "You know it isn't necessary? Right?" She was amused that he would ask for the quiet room.

He stroked her cheek and kissed her softly. "Yes, I know but it is more fun this way. The receptionist thinks we are having an affair. Or that we are going to engage in wild kinky sex."

Susan returned his smile and added, "I seriously can't imagine that she could picture the kind of time I think we are going to have."

Patrick smiled warmly, took her arm, and guided her as they walked to the rather old-fashioned, but stylish, mirrored, art deco elevator. The door juddered slightly as it opened with an old world ting. They entered and Patrick confidently pressed the floor button. There was a delay, as the elevator seemed to be thinking about the instruction. Patrick was just about to press the button again, when the door came to life and slid closed.

They were the sole occupants of the elevator. Susan didn't want to waste a precious second of their time together. She moved closer to Patrick. She felt so nurtured. Patrick had given her the confidence to be happy with who she was. He had given her the freedom to be happy with her own body and with her own desires. He was the first man who didn't make her feel strange for wanting to give herself so completely to a man and she loved him for it. Looking into his eyes she said, "With all my heart I love you."

They sank into a warm loving embrace. His arms surrounded her, held her securely. His protective manliness enveloped her and made her tingle from head to toe as their lips came together. She held him tightly, feeling him pull her body closer to his. She was aware of the wetness of her panties as his thigh pressed between her legs. She pressed herself against his leg relishing the pressure. Her hands gripped his ass. She was aware of the tactile feeling beneath her hands, as she squeezed. She could feel the fabric of his trousers and then the solid, firmness of him beneath. She pulled him even closer, loving the hard masculine feel of his body. She could feel his erection pressing hard against her yielding flesh.

She felt his ardent tongue probe her lips, which parted for him. She surrendered willingly. His insistent tongue ravaged her; she gave him full access to her mouth, thinking that soon he would take possession of her body.

He could feel her tremble as he held her in his arms. She was so small and delicate, like a flower, wafting in a warm summer breeze yet he knew from previous encounters, how strong she was. From their many times together he knew how submissive she was, but her enthusiasm for their embrace, her grip on his ass and her breathiness as they kissed reminded him she was no passive love partner. He could feel her passion and loved that her fervor matched his own.

The gap between their meetings had been too long. He thought of the long nights alone, joined by a phone line that united them across the miles. They had developed this easy rapport over the years. He loved the openness that had developed between them and their ability to share the most intimate details of their fantasies.

He thought back to the early days of their relationship. They had been friends for a long time before things had become sexual. Their meetings had been friendly in the beginning. Candlelight dinners, movies, the theatre, their tastes had been well matched. The more they had gotten to know each other, the more they found they had in common and each new commonality brought them closer.

He had surprised himself, by how tentative he had been, when it had come to broaching the subject of sex with Susan. It had not been because of a lack of desire, but more the worry of risking a friendship. In Susan, he had found a true soul mate, someone who made him happy and he'd been loathe to risk what they had. He had been relieved to find that Susan had shared the same worry. With the mutual fear discussed, there had followed a night of sensitive, tender lovemaking.

After this most tentative of starts, he had been surprised by how quickly and how easily they had been able to communicate their innermost thoughts. First, it had been a total intimacy of minds, talking about fantasies, breaking down the social taboos, his need to control, hers to submit. He loved their sheer willingness to explore every topic under the sun. They talked of her desire to be restrained and their mutual willingness to explore things they had never explored before. They discussed water sports, corporal punishment and anal sex, in a way that was unashamed and unreserved.

As their relationship grew over the months and years, his love for her had deepened. Like two romantic pioneers, their exploration had taken them to new heights.

The only thing that stood between them was their lifestyles and their career choices, but those things fragmented their lives. There were the wonderful loving moments, but they were segmented between the disagreeable breaks apart. The desire to be together was strong and this had led to an upside to the breaks, the phone calls.

During their late night phone trysts they had explored their fantasies, talking of soft tender times, of kisses, hugs and cuddles, while his hands stroked his penis and he listened to her sighs and gasps as he imagined her fingers playing in her soft silken crease. Their erotic chats covered the spectrum of desires and tastes, from the soft to the raw. They talked into the early hours, husky voices whispering hard-edged fantasies of BDSM, bondage, toys and clamps. He remembered heated voices close to climax, uttering their love within the framework of domination and submission as they enjoyed the ultimate surrender of one to the other in a glorious power exchange.

They had explored the subject of domination and submission on many occasions. He knew she loved the intense excitement and heightened emotional states it brought because of the passionate way she described the scenes of her fantasies. He remembered the husky tone of her voice as she had described the humiliation of being exhibited in public, the lusty way she depicted the way she wanted him to tie her down to the bed, and the way she willingly gave her body to him. When she spoke of her submission, she did so joyously and with unashamed enthusiasm. He remembered slowly stroking his penis, on these occasions, as she told him how she wanted to be used, how she wanted to be spanked and kissed. He remembered the intensity of the orgasms, his ears ringing with her gravelly voice, as she described how she longed to be fucked, by his hard cock, how she wanted to feel him inside her hot pussy, how she ached to take him in her tight ass. As he listened to her voice on the other end of the telephone line, he would often hear her cum for him, his own passionate moans pushing her to climax.

It had made him feel honored to be so trusted by her. He also found that level of trust a very strong aphrodisiac.

Their power exchange had been the subject of their last phone call, which had lasted into the small hours of the morning. In that steamy night's chat, they had explored the idea of her total submission to his every whim, to his total control. It had started softly and slowly, as most of their encounters did. He sat on the edge of his bed wrapped comfortably in his thick cotton-toweling robe. He had adjusted the lights, darkening the room. The phone connection made, he sank back onto the bed, making himself comfortable.

"How are you tonight?" he said longing to hear her voice.

"I'm fine, it has been a long day, it is nice to unwind, and it's lovely to hear your voice."

He figured that she must have had a long day, as there was tiredness in her voice, but it sounded sweet to his ears. "What have you been doing to get ready for our conversation?"

There was a brief pause. He pictured her playing with her earlobe, as she often did when she was getting what she wanted to say straight in her own mind before speaking the words aloud. "I have had a long bath, washed my hair. I shaved myself smooth for you, the way you like me."

There was another pause. He knew she wanted his

approval and he answered with a simple, "You are a good girl, that pleases me." The words were simple but the meaning was deep, his possession of her, him giving approval.

He got as much from it as she did, he loved having someone who needed his praise. He never failed to get a buzz from that. He was the dominant, though it had not escaped him that it had been Susan that had initiated her surrender rather than he who had asked for it. He loved her submissive nature. It was like they were two halves of the same coin and he would never forget that her submission was a beautiful gift.

She continued, "After I dried myself I put on the black lace bra and panties you brought back from your last trip to Europe." There was a pause, which Patrick filled with a grunt of approval. "And my stockings and the garter belt you like me to wear… I hope you approve?"

He knew that she already knew the answer to that question, but he filled in the blank. "Yes I totally approve. It pleases me greatly." He loved the feeling of power and the intense feeling of being in total control. Yes, she was doing what he asked, but she was doing it for the sole purpose of giving him pleasure. He pictured her there dressed for him, dressed for his inspection. His erection rose from beneath the cotton of his toweling robe and he began to toy with the thickening flesh. "What are you doing right now?" He listened intently for the reply.

"I am on the bed, with all my toys around me, waiting for your command. What would you have your humble servant do to please you?"

He heard her voice calm, yet a little huskier than normal. He heard the arousal in her words. He found her excitement stimulating his own thoughts of carnal pleasure. "It would please me if you would feel your breasts for me. Feel their weight. Feel the size and shape." He left little pauses, where he listened for her sighs, listened to the soundscape, which painted his own mental picture of what she was doing. All the while he spoke his own deft fingers stroked, enough to keep him stimulated, but not enough to take his mind of the most important thing, Susan. "Feel your nipples for me please."

"Yes Sir."

He heard her sigh a little. "Does that feel nice?"

"Yes Sir, thank you Sir."

"You are most welcome my pet. Squeeze a little harder for me please." He heard her sigh turn slowly to a moan as he pictured the increase of pressure. In his mind's eye, he could see her back arch. "A little more." Over the phone came a little gasp of air. He paused, "And relax…." There was an audible exhale. "How do you feel?"

Her voice was slow and husky, "Wonderful, thank you Sir"

By her tone, he could tell that she was all right. They had been having sexual encounters on the phone for some time and he had always followed each session with asking how it was for her. He prided himself on the fact that he could hear in each inflection of her voice, her precise state of mind, a thing that some couples didn't enjoy in face-to-face meetings. He could tell her state of arousal by the pace of her breathing. To be able to enjoy this connection from separate corners of the globe was truly an incredible thing.

"I am very pleased and proud of you."

"Thank you Sir."

Patrick rubbed a tear of pre-cum off his penis, with his thumb and licked it, picturing Susan tasting him. "Are you wet my pet?"

"Yes Sir, very wet and all in your honor my master."

He remembered how difficult it had been, to get Susan to the point where she could vocalize her erotic thoughts. He recalled her tentative steps and the way he had encouraged her baby steps. Through the vocabulary of the medical words for their genitalia to the more base Anglo-Saxon, it had been a long journey through the briar patch of sensibilities, but by and by, he had made her feel comfortable using profanities. He wanted her to be able to describe the act she wanted to experience. He was pleased with the progress she had made and found it an immense turn on to hear her talking dirty. There was something delicious about hearing such dirty words, from such a tender lady.

"I would like you to stroke your panties between your labia," he paused picturing the scene. "Run your finger along your slit for me please, from your clit to your pussy." He paused allowing time for the action. "And back again." Another pause. "Feel good?"

Her only reply was a "hmmmmmmm" like a cat that had gotten the cream.

It gave him pleasure to be the one to give her pleasure, to be in control of the scene, making this happen. "Press a little harder my pet. Push your panties harder against your pussy for me." Her moan told him she was complying with the instruction. "A little harder." He paused to make a space for her moan, which followed. He could tell by the pitch she was close to climax. He wanted her to cum, yet wanted the bittersweet tension to continue. "I would like you to stop please."

There was no disguising the disappointment in her voice. "Yes Sir."

Though he knew she was disappointed not to cum he also knew she would be lifted to new heights by playing this tantalizing game of tease and denial. The power to do this, to control this personal activity with his words, to be the one whose command would grant or deny her orgasm was a powerful aphrodisiac. He felt privileged, that she had trusted him enough to give him this power over her body, to relinquish her self-will.

"Spread your legs for me please," he paused for the task. "I want you to feel the nylon of your stockings, feel the sheer material. I want you to feel it with my hands, feel it as if I were there with you now. Feel the warmth of your hand on your leg. Imagine me looking down on you, your legs spread. Open. Wet." He paused for dramatic effect. "I want to spank you." He knew she was excited by being spanked, I want you to ask me."

There was no hesitation, but a tremble of desire in her voice "Please Sir, would you do the honor of spanking me?"

"It would give me great pleasure, where would you like me to spank you?" He squeezed his cock in anticipation of her words.

"My body is yours to do with as you will."

Her words were music to his ears, and were he a lesser man he would have cum there and then he was so excited. "I wish to spank your pussy." He paused to let his words sink in. "Three good ones, on my command please." He paused to let her anticipation build. "One!" There was a resounding smack and the sound of her sucking in her breath, a sound he echoed. "Two!" The smack sounded even harder, so was her indrawn breath and his response. "Make the last one nice for me!" The third crack was louder still, and so was his appreciative sigh. "God I am hungry for you"

"Sir I am hungry for you. Fuck me please. Please Sir. I need you now!"

Her voice held desperation and he was torn between giving her what she craved and his need to control her. His own voice trembled a little, giving away the fact that his own hand was gripping, slowly stroking, and that his own climax could be hastened very easily. He exercised the same restraint with himself as he did with his lady.

"You have the phallus? The pink one?" They had bought the toy together on a stopover in Baltimore, and the vibrator was the size and thickness of his own penis.

"Yes I have it right here, Sir." Her voice was keen with anticipation, hot with hunger.

"Kiss the tip for me please." He could hear the moist sound of her lips opening, the noise of her anointing the phallus. His own penis ached for release, yet he knew he would wait until he had her orgasmic cry.

"I would like you to feel the size and shape." His ears listened to the soundscape. "Know I am going to fuck you long and hard," he heard her muffled moan. "Now I want you to take my cock from your lips, I want you to pull your panties aside, I want you to put the head of my penis to your nether lips." Again, he paused, to give her time to comply. "It would please me if you would slide it up inside." Down the phone came her moans and sighs as the phallus was buried deeply. "Your time has come. Time again to ask for what you want."

"If it pleases you Sir, I give myself to you, I need you. Please Sir, please Sir have the body I offer you. Fuck me now! Please Sir! Fuck me now!"

He heard the urgency in her words and knew she had waited quite long enough. "Turn on the vibrator please." He could hear the faint buzz in the background. "Slowly, very slowly, I want you to slide it in and out." Although miles separated them, her pants of pleasure matched his own, as he stroked his cock to the same rhythm. They were one beneath the stars.

"I want you to feel every inch. All the way in, all the way out." He listened for her response, and was rewarded with her sighs and moans of exertion. He felt his own crisis quickening. "Harder! My pet, harder!" Her moans and breaths shortened. He gripped his cock tight, picturing it in her silken sheath. He knew she must hear the strain in his voice. "Harder! Faster!"

"Please Sir... May I..."

He could hear her at the very brink of climax. His pause now was excruciating for them both.

"Please!"

"Yes… My pet you may…" His words gave him power, that power made him feel exultant to be the one to grant pleasure. His grip around his penis tightened, his own need called. He found his pulse racing; the sound of her climax filled his head. In his mind, he was right there, right with her, his cock filling her, his weight pinning her to the bed, his cum surging into her rather than onto his stomach.

He lay there panting, listening to her heavy breathing, on the other end of the phone. Her breaths came in short gasps.

He felt a profound sense of wellbeing. He was calm and relaxed. He listened quietly, as her breathing became less labored, as she began to relax. He could almost hear the ripples of orgasm subsiding

"Are you ok?" He felt the ripples of his climax slowly dissipating.

"I feel wonderful."

He loved that she sounded as chilled-out as he felt. "I am pleased… You sounded as if you needed that?" He waited a moment. "It gave me great pleasure, to hear you cum."

"Thank you Sir. I did need to cum. I have been wound up all day." Her voice stopped, as if contemplating what to say next. "I can't wait for tomorrow, I want to serve you in the flesh. I want to feel you inside me. I want to be yours. All yours." Her pause made him hungry for her next words, "Your requests for tomorrow, Sir? How can I serve you? Make it better for you?"

He had most of the following day mapped out in his mind. "I would like you to wear those new fitted panties I sent you." He listened intently for her reply.

"Hmmmmm. Goodness, that will be interesting. Another first. Will there be any other instructions, Sir?"

"Only for you to dress to please me."

"That goes without saying, my sweet master. You are always in my mind when I dress. It might be the airline on show, but it is you next to my skin."

Their words were soft like summer rain, their chat felt like the warm cuddle following lovemaking. Their tireless conversation carried on long into the morning.

In the hours he waited for her, thoughts of her had

consumed him. He had replayed the phone call in his mind over and over and it had fuelled his hunger. His penis had never really softened from waking this morning. The whole subject of power exchange was on his mind. He was dominant, but his power carried with it responsibilities, her safety, and her pleasure. He loved her dearly and wanted to be the one to give her all she needed.

The elevator went up smoothly, but all that mattered to Susan was the closeness of her master, his warmth, his presence, his scent. Her tongue danced with his, a passionate tango. She couldn't help thinking of the afternoon of sensual delights, ahead. She remembered the phone calls and e-mails over the last week that had led them both to this. Her body tingled with excitement. She could not wait to get to the room.

Last night's call had fuelled one of the most powerful orgasms she had ever experienced. His silken voice had played in her mind, painting erotic scenes for her pleasure. While his words had stirred her emotions with the plans for this day, her fingers had strummed her sensitive kernel of desire. She was excited hearing his plans, the silken ties, the toys, and instructions for her clothing. She loved that he cared so much that he would plan her life in such detail. It made her feel wanted.

The stream of eroticism filled her mind as their tongues danced. She was so aroused, she felt that she could almost cum, right here and now. She loved the feel of his hard body, the penetrating kiss, his physical presence, pressed tight up against her. In her mind, she recalled her passionate gasps down the phone last night, the way she had surrendered herself as Patrick listened.

The feel of his erection brought her back into the present and made her aware of his hardness, and her own wetness, the fact that her body was ready and willing to serve.

Their kiss and embrace ended reluctantly as the elevator clattered to a halt. The bright little bell chimed and the door opened shakily.

They breezed down the corridor of the fourth floor, with the haste of teenage lovers. Susan shared every bit of Patrick's hunger. She yearned to get to the privacy of their hotel room, to give herself to the man she loved.

Chapter Three

Time is at Hand

Patrick crossed the room, the carpet muffling his footsteps. "I think it best to save the food until later, but a glass of bubbly would be nice." He leaned close and whispered in her ear, "May I have your watch? How much time do we have?"

Susan unfastened the watch's wrist strap. "I have to check in at 2:30, so we have about an hour before I have to leave."

Patrick noticed that the z engraved on the back of the watch had left a mark on her wrist. He lifted her hand to his lips and kissed the mark. "An hour is more than enough time, almost an eternity." He looked into her eyes, smiled and kissed her on the lips.

Susan thought of the time that stretched before them, her mind going back to the night before and the plans they had made for this time they would have together. She was suddenly very aware of the two phalluses buried deeply within her and the now insistent throbbing of her clit. She imagined the throbbing as the tick-tock of her body clock. She returned his smile and his kiss and then handed the watch to him. "Yes an eternity."

She had conquered all doubts, exceeded her own expectations and fulfilled her master's task. The feeling of elation welled up inside her filling her heart with happiness and excitement.

Looking forward, but using her peripheral vision, she followed Patrick around the room.

The room had the soft scent of jasmine and the temperature was just right, neither too cool nor too stuffy. She stood quietly, her eyes following her master, as he moved smoothly, almost catlike, around the room. She admired his athletic, muscular build beneath his smart attire and found herself wondering what was going through his mind. How would he want to start? The thought made her vagina and anal muscles contract, making the dildos move inside her. The sensation made her breathing heavier and her heart beat faster.

He took his own watch from his pocket and flipped the case open. The time pieces were in perfect sync, the hands locked together. Even the second hands were in perfect sync, sweeping to the top of the hour. 56, 57, 58, 59, then both said one o'clock as he put the watches together on the bedside dresser. After looking at the timepieces for a moment, he unbuttoned his waistcoat, slipped it from his shoulders and hung it across the back of a chair.

Although he was to her side, and she continued to look forward, he was clearly visible.

Susan stood passively and watched. He moved freely and easily. Smoothly. There was something erotic about the way he moved, the way his erection pressed against his pants. The ease of his movements and his authority made her feel secure in his presence.

She found herself biting her lower lip, as she admired the broadness of his chest and shoulders, as he unbuttoned his vest and slipped it smoothly from his shoulders. She watched as his lean fingers worked over the knot of his tie. It was all part of a ritual. There was a sense that he was preparing himself for her, stripping to get down to business. Susan turned her head slightly to get a better look. She loved watching the man she loved stripping, just for her, and she didn't want to miss a thing.

Her greedy eyes took in this voyeuristic scene, her mind racing, her body tingling with enjoyment at his slow deliberate performance. She mentally licked each morsel of newly exposed flesh, and the thought of oral homage made her body ache with hunger.

She relished the naughty way it made her feel watching someone else take off their clothes. She felt the heat of desire spreading rhythmically from the heart of her sex, to her outer extremities. The throb between her legs more insistent now. She became aware of the wetness between her thighs as a light whisper of cool air chilled her leg. Her gaze flicked from Patrick momentarily, as she caught a glimpse of her body in the bedroom mirror. The flush of desire on her cheeks and chest was unmistakable. Seeing her own arousal made her feel empowered. Not that she was in control of the situation but that she was in control of her body. She had felt her orgasm building from the moment she had first held him in her arms and yet she had held back the tide.

Her glimpse in the mirror had taken a fraction of a second and now she fixed her attention firmly on her lover. His body as he stripped was lean and hard, tight buttocks and manly flesh, kempt and smooth, firm and erect. She ached to have the phalluses that held her passages open, replaced by his manhood. Her hunger churned like a pan of milk on a stove, the foam rising, as it comes to the boil. Her desire wanting to boil over, yet she was kept on simmer, kept from release. God she *wanted* him!

Patrick thumbed apart his tie, flicking open his top button and pulling his tie free of his collar. As he did, he looked at Susan. He lusted after her body, there was no doubt of that, but he loved her, truly loved her for all she was, her keen mind, her sharp wit. All that she was brought joy to his life.

His hand delved into his pocket drawing out the loose change in his cupped fingers and scattering the small number of coins on the dresser. The elegant watches caught his eye.

They lay side by side on the dresser. The two timepieces were different in many ways, hers so dainty and feminine, his all together more robust, business like and masculine. There were many ways they were the same too, the warm luster of the rose gold, the faces of the watches were identical in style, the numerals and hands the same rather ornate Arabic design. He smiled with satisfaction, at the second hands ticking in unison. He considered the watches two peas in a pod, as he and Susan were.

His glance traveled to Susan's wrist, and he noticed the Z was slowly fading. It resembled a small brand, and it pleased him to think, that when she wore the watch the emblem pressing into her skin was a physical symbol of their love and devotion.

He thought about how emotionally connected they were, the way that she would say something he was thinking, the way she would anticipate his needs, and the way he anticipated hers. When they walked, their strides matched, just as the watches were physically together. Patrick's mind slipped back to the time when they had come across the shop where they had purchased the watches.

It was in the older quarter of the city, an area that looked a bit down at heel. They had wandered into this part of town by accident, wandering from the more trendy Latin Quarter, looking for an interesting restaurant for a lunchtime tryst. Patrick remembered her concern.

"I don't really feel comfortable. Shouldn't we go back?" Her manner had been twitchy.

He had smiled reassuringly into her wider than normal pale green eyes and held her hand. "I wouldn't want to be wandering here at night, but I think it is ok, it looks kind of interesting." He'd made a few loose hand gestures toward the slightly quirky buildings. "I don't think it would hurt to look about a bit. Okay?"

Reassured by his confidence, she'd smiled. "Okay. It does look kind of interesting."

The buildings looked as if they had been built at different times. They all looked old, but some looked a lot older than others. Some looked cared for and lived in, but others had windows that had been unwashed for many years, with net curtains that were tattered and torn. Patrick speculated about the potential number of rats lurking just out of sight.

Hand in hand, they walked down the slightly uneven cobbled street. All around were tightly packed shops and houses with small panes of bull's eye glass in wooden frames that needed attention. The air was musky with the scent of old and rotting wood.

Patrick with his business head on, made a mental note that the area was prime for redevelopment. As quickly as the thought popped into his mind, his focus drifted back to the slightly crooked doors, with flaking paint. Little curiosity shops, that surely could not make a living in this day and age. Yet here they were a small baker, bread on display, an ironmongers shop, with boxes of screws and a scattering of tools on display. His nostrils caught the delicate sent of summer flowers. Hand in hand, they turned the corner and before them was a small florists shop. He smiled and kissed Susan, breaking their handhold to pop inside. He re-emerged a few seconds later with a single rose, which he presented to Susan. "A rose for my rose."

Susan lifted her head from smelling the rose, to catch his warm loving gaze.

He looked into her eyes and delighted at the sight of her smile. He felt her squeeze his hand, then her soft body pressed into his. He loved to have her so close to him, soft, yielding. It was a joy to have her firm breasts pressed into his chest and to feel her soft lips on his cheek, before she whispered a soft, "Thank you," in his ear.

Patrick caught a glimpse of an old shop, tucked away in a side alley. Something he could not explain drew him to it. As they approached, the old frontage blended in with its surroundings. A small faded sign in the window read, "Guild of Goldsmiths, jewelry made to order." The window display was sparse, yet the items on display were exquisite, small broaches on burgundy velvet cushions, rings displayed hung from small branches on a small Z shaped tree, which was the centerpiece of the display. He noticed and was intrigued that the faded sign above the shop said the Crimson Z, a tie in with the Z shaped tree in the window, he was sure. The whole display was simple but very effective. There was a dusty feel to it, yet the gold caught the light, as if it had been polished just that morning.

"We should have a look inside," Patrick said stepping forward. Something in Susan's manner gave him the feeling that she was a little resistant. It was the way she hung back, where she was normally a stride forward. Patrick looked at her quizzically and asked, "Is there a problem?"

She squeezed his hand. "I don't know. It looks a bit creepy."

He smiled. "Come on, what have we got to lose? It looks interesting." He squeezed her hand encouragingly. "We might find a little something inside."

He felt her resistance melt as they opened the door. As they entered the shop, a small bell tinkled. He squinted as his eyes became accustomed to the dimly lit shop. He was aware of a slightly musty, damp smell, invading his nostrils as he looked around the outside of the room. Small, colored glass shaded wall lights illuminated the rough wooden floorboards that creaked beneath their feet. Old-fashioned glass display cases displayed an array of pretty trinkets on miniature stands. The displays had the same theme as the front window, small burgundy velvet cushions, all of which showed off the beautiful craftsmanship of the pieces displayed on them. There was something very quaint about the displays, anachronistic, out of step, a total contrast to more modern shops. Patrick liked the old world feel.

Behind the counter was a long thin metal stand. It was decorative as was the cage that hung from it. The whole thing looked very old and rather dusty. It was not instantly noticeable, but in the corner was a small white bird. It only made a small amount of noise, as it hopped from its perch to the side of the cage and back. He switched his attention to the rest of the shop, which appeared empty.

On the front counter, there was a gold pocket watch the back of the case open, the skeleton of its works smoothly ticking away. Something about the timepiece caught Patrick's eye. Even from a distance, the solid look of the case made it look dependable, and as he got closer, quality exuded from the chronometer. The skill that had gone into the engraving was truly lovely, clean and precise.

He moved closer still to admire the workmanship. It was as beautiful as it was skillfully engineered. He had always loved timepieces and in the top drawer of his dressing table, there was a rather large collection. He had in his possession all manner of watches, from fine dress watches, designer pieces and a number of sports clocks, even a rather dated digital watch from the 1970's. This pocket watch was something very special, truly class, a mark of status, a symbol of success and an object that he now very much wanted to own.

He was just about to touch the precious metal, when a strongly accented voice came from somewhere behind him.

"Beautiful, isn't it Sir? Do you think I might be of service, Sir?"

Both Patrick and Susan were startled by the unexpected appearance of the well-built, bearded man. His voice was deep, calm, and measured. "I am sorry if I startled you, please allow me to introduce, myself. I am Zachariah. Welcome to my humble establishment."

Patrick composed himself and replied "Thank you. You have an interesting shop."

Zachariah meshed his fingers together and gave a curious nod of the head. "I like to think we have the things that people are looking for and of course for special customers, I am happy to make that special item." The old man walked slowly round to the other side of the counter. He moved confidently and with grace, for a man of his years. "I can see you have an eye for timepieces," Zachariah said as he picked up the pocket watch and handed it to Patrick. "Exquisite isn't it?"

Patrick stroked the engraving turning the watch in his hand stroking the sensually decorated Z on the back.

Zachariah slowly continued. "I sense that time is an issue? An issue for you both, maybe? Time I suppose is a concern for us all, but I feel it is especially so for both of you."

As he put his arm around Susan's shoulders, Patrick looked down to find her looking up at him. Her slightly furrowed brow echoed his own feeling of unease. His hand moved from her shoulders to stroke her hair reassuringly. It was in this act of soothing her, he felt easier about the situation himself. He felt as if Zachariah just knew his, their, thoughts. He found that a very spooky thing, but there seemed to be nothing sinister about the old man. Looking at the expression on his lover's face, he could see she was thinking the same thing he was. Like him, she seemed less troubled about the situation.

Zachariah seemed happy with the moment's silence. "Time is a troublesome thing in this day and age; we never seem to have enough of it. Don't you agree?"

Patrick was struck by his words, they were so perceptive. "Yes, I think you are right," he answered simply. Maybe it was the thoughts of time, the feeling that there was never enough of it, or that time was running out that gave him his affinity to own and collect timepieces. He had a collection of over thirty, each unique in its own right. Time was always the issue and he heard the jeweler's words in his head. *Time is a troublesome thing in this day and age, we never seem to have enough of it.*

Patrick rolled the watch in his hand. Both sides were beautifully engraved there was a tactile knurling around the edge to stop it slipping from his hand. It was well thought out, practical, and beautifully decorative. The whole feel of this pocket watch was so right. Its weight was substantial yet not too heavy. The style was old world, yet not dated. He thought classic would be a fair description. He showed the timepiece to Susan, who seemed as fascinated by the watch as he was. "How much, would a watch such as this cost?"

The large man looked deep into Patrick's eyes. "One thing you must consider when buying such a watch, is that it is not just a trinket. This is a serious watch for a serious man. In buying this watch, you will see your life in a new way. Maybe you will worry less about the ticking of the clock, and more about what is important to you when filling the hours." Zachariah's eyes still had a spark of youth, though his age showed in his body and more especially in his slightly gnarled hands. "If you don't mind me making the observation Sir, price is not the issue. It is more a case of if you are ready to make this purchase, more a case of if the time is right."

The corner of his mouth curled into a charming smile. It amused Patrick that Zachariah seemed to know him so well. He realized that his clothes showed him to be financially buoyant. He ran his hand across his tailored trousers. He wasn't comfortable in jeans.

Zachariah pulled himself straight to his full height, which Patrick judged to be a little under six feet. He looked an imposing character in his black suit in the Hasidic tradition. He wore no tie but a white shirt with the top button done up. His long beard was flecked grey as was his long hair, which contained more salt than pepper.

Patrick reflected that the jeweler must have been even more impressive as a young man, yet even now, there was something timeless about him. He had a quiet strength and power that made him seem like the sort of man you would be unwise to get on the wrong side of.

Patrick turned his attention back to the watch. He knew

he would have to buy this watch.

"I can see, you have made up your mind, and may I say Sir you have made the right decision. You will not regret it." The goldsmith smiled broadly. "I also have a suggestion for the lady." He took from his pocket a small thin lady's dress watch. "I know it is rather presumptive of me," he passed the watch to Susan, "but this rather suits you and I think the two watches will keep perfect time together."

Although the lady's wristwatch was smaller and more delicate in style, it closely resembled the pocket watch. It carried the same engraving. On the back, there was the same stylized letter z. It was plain to see that the watches had the same maker.

Patrick looked at Susan. It was obvious she was taken with the watch. All seemed right. Perfect timing he thought, in every sense of the expression. "Thank you, we will take them," he announced, offering his hand to shake on the deal.

The jeweler took his hand and shook it with an honest, trustworthy grip "The watches are not quite finished. I need to finish them both off. They need to be tuned to run perfectly together. I would like to customize them. This might sound a tad bizarre but I like these things to be personalized to the individuals buying them." The large man paused and looked at the couple before him. "Normally I get what I need by subterfuge, but I can see you are direct people, so I will ask outright. I would like a tiny sample of your blood, just the merest smidge. Call it the eccentric nature of an old man." He shrugged. "It is the belief of my people that the mixing of blood from a loving couple will bind them in time." The old man paused, he seemed to have a hesitant look on his face, as if there was something he should say, but was debating in his own mind whether to say it or not. After his deliberation he went on, "There must also be added a little blood from an innocent, this will blend the whole elixir together."

Patrick raised an eyebrow, "An innocent?" He paused to

see if the old man might offer further insight to the source of the innocent blood, but none was forthcoming. "Are we talking sacrificial virgins?"

The jeweler smiled, obviously amused by the suggestion. There was a hint of a stifled laugh in his voice when he replied. "No, I don't think we need to go quite that far on this occasion.

Patrick looked at Susan, feeling a little foolish about bringing up the subject of virgins. She gave him a small shrug and a rather skeptical look, yet with a smile and a second shrug agreed. He looked on as she offered the goldsmith her hand and saw her wince as the pin pricked the end of her thumb. Patrick followed and a tiny sample of his blood was taken.

Zachariah smiled and nodded courteously. "Thank you, the final procedure will take about thirty minutes, you may wait if you wish, or return later."

Patrick looked at Susan to see if she had a preference. Not seeing any in her expression, he answered, "If it is ok we will wait."

"Would you care for some tea while you wait?"

Having guided Susan to the more comfortable of the two chairs, Patrick carefully eased himself onto the remaining, rather rickety seat. He watched the hands of the old grandfather clock, heard its steady tick and silently contemplated the nature of time. Time, he thought, was an unusual commodity. In some respects like a liquid, it flows. Sometimes it feels like it is still and calm, other times it runs like a waterfall down a mountain. He considered how time felt, right then and there. The wait felt like laying in a warm bath, or like being in a small boat on a calm lake, no pressure, time to think and ponder, a wonderful contrast to his usual, *not a minute to spare* feeling, which was vaguely reminiscent of him feeling like a salmon swimming against the tide. The grandfather clock ticked on, the hands slowly moving around the face. He checked his own wristwatch, which said the same time to the second. He thought that strange.

The relentless tick of the old wooden case clock measured out the segments of time and chimed for the half hour. Patrick looked at his watch, which told him that thirty minutes had passed. In a way thirty minutes felt about right, but in other ways it felt as if he had been waiting all day. In other ways, it felt like it had been only a matter of seconds. Patrick turned to find Susan looking equally disorientated. A shrill noise from the back of the shop focused him and his mind raced as he considered what would make a noise like that. His eyes flicked around the room and landed on the cage. It was now empty. He frantically recalled the conversation about innocent blood. He felt a little sick. Surely not? A tang of guilt gripped him. The bird! Oh Christ no! Not the bird!

Seconds later, Zachariah emerged smiling, bird alive and well on his finger. His old hand fiddled with the latch on the door of the cage. Once opened the bird fluttered inside none the worse for whatever ordeal it may have suffered. The old man turned to Patrick a knowing smirk on his face. "Surely you didn't think I would harm the creature?"

The goldsmith presented them with their watches. The deal was struck with a final handshake as the money changed hands.

Zachariah escorted them to the door. "What has gone on here is more than a simple transaction," his voice had been warm and friendly. "What we have here is a bond. I hope very much that you will come back and see me again."

As they left the shop, Patrick turned and shook Zachariah's hand again. "Yes, we will be back." The idea of having an engagement ring made by the craftsman came into his mind. The idea of proposing to Susan was not a new idea, but the notion of the ring seemed to come from nowhere.

"Rings are one of my specialties," Zachariah said a twinkle in his eye.

Patrick smiled. *How the hell had he known he was thinking*

that?

A glint of light from the watches brought Patrick's thoughts back to the hotel room, and he looked directly at Susan. She looked magnificent. His gaze followed her long, straight, stockinged legs then dipped to her shoes. Lifting his gaze, he followed the fine lines of her calves, her knees and thighs, held tight together. His gaze paused at the stocking tops. He loved the way the nylon changed color in the two bands at the top. Then his gaze lifted a little higher to the harness that held the dildos in place. He clenched his own buttocks, trying to imagine how Susan must feel, invaded, possessed. He felt his penis twitch. His eyes moved upwards across her pleasantly rounded belly, over the faint outline of ribs, to her ripe breasts, to rest on her proud hard nipples. His thoughts were momentarily interrupted by the insistent pulse in his groin, his body's call to make itself heard. He returned his focus to Susan, his eyes following up her body, up her beautiful innocent face framed by long, beautiful, flowing hair that cascaded down onto her shoulders. His animal urges were calling him and he knew the time drew near to consummate their tryst, flesh to flesh.

Chapter Four

Cometh the Hour

Susan was watching him, as he placed the timepieces on the bedside cabinet. She stood, aware of her body, her nerve endings alive. She could feel her own heart beating, the pulse echoing throughout her body. A wisp of cool air brushed her hard nipples and moist labia. Her fingertips trembled. Her eyes were glued to his, hungrily anticipating his first command. She knew he never commanded her to do things, instead he made requests, requests she longed to fulfill.

He could see her need. Her arousal was undeniable. He could see the smoldering fire of desire in her dilated pupils, pouting lips, the flush of pink over her cheeks and chest, and the deep color of her areolas and tight erect nipples. His ravenous gaze traveled down her lithe body. The blush of desire washed over her abdomen, down to her moistened thighs.

It was clear that her need matched his own. He licked his lips, as he looked at her nubile frame, wanting her and loving her for the submission that she so freely gave him. His hand in his pocket stroked his painfully erect penis. "My pet, would you come to me, please."

She had hungrily anticipated his first command and she responded quickly, moving swiftly to his side. His voice was measured and calm and his words sent a tingle down her spine. She yearned to give herself to him completely and for him to take her wholly. She loved him so entirely that in her submission she freely gave him all she was.

She loved the way he used the power she gave him. In giving her total submission to this one man, she felt complete, not just in a physical way, but in a deep emotional way, as if she was giving him her very soul. Giving her master the power made her feel enriched, confident in her love for him and in his love for her. Her trust in him was absolute.

The nerve endings in her skin bristled as her mind raced, a million questions sprang up. What would happen? How would he use her? She felt her heart pound in the cage of her chest, the same pulse echoed constantly around her engorged clit and around the two phalluses.

As she crossed the carpeted floor to her beloved master, she was intensely aware of the two phalluses moving inside her. It was as if he was already inside her, his cock fucking her as she moved. The sensation wasn't new. It had been there since she'd inserted them, but now with this long build up, the feeling was even more intense.

Giving herself to him felt so right, so good, as if she had been born for this purpose.

In her mind, she wanted more. But could she live this intensely all the time? What would it be like to serve Patrick 24/7? Would he want her that way, all the time? She dismissed that thought, pushing it down deep inside herself. Serving Patrick 24/7 wasn't possible. They both had demanding careers that took them in opposite directions for long stretches of time. But in spite of the little voice that told her it wasn't possible, she felt a strong drive to find out what a life of submission to Patrick would be like.

She broke from her inner thoughts to catch a glimpse of the warmth of Patrick's smile and felt her heart soar.

Patrick stroked his hand delicately through her hair. The feel of her hair gave him great pleasure. The silky fibers slipping through his fingers were so sensual. His eyes fixed on hers, "Your last chance, my pet, from this point on you will be my possession to do with as I see fit. Do you submit?"

Patrick looked into her eyes and saw his intensity mirrored in her eyes.

She smiled and replied, "With all my heart, I submit to you."

Her words flowed over him like a summer breeze on a hot day. Her gift to him was more precious than anything in the world. His heart lifted to new heights as the intoxicating power she bestowed on him surged through him. He bristled with excitement the hairs on the back of his neck standing as erect as his penis. He was so proud of her, ecstatically empowered by the trust she gave him so freely.

He looked deeply into her pale green eyes, "What we will do here today will be for our mutual pleasure."

The smile and slow deliberate nod was her reply.

"Very well my pet." The merest touch to her head indicated he wanted her to kneel and without hesitation, she complied.

He felt his own pulse, felt the blood surging through his veins. He buzzed. The control he had over her made him tingle, as if electricity was passing through his body. The crush of complex emotions raging through him made him feel a little light headed, but it was a magnificent feeling.

It would have been easy to use the power she had given him to satisfy his own carnal lust, but he knew he had to exercise restraint. He had responsibilities to Susan. She trusted him, and he would live up to the trust she had placed in him.

He hungered for her. He felt a physical ache deep within, an ache that made him want to have her there and then, yet his self control and his love for her made him want to give her as much pleasure as he wanted for himself. Aware of all of this, he would not let his hunger to sate his own desires overshadow his power to be the giver of pleasure.

It gave him enormous satisfaction to be the one who gave. He had never seen that as being at odds with his natural dominance. It felt right and natural to give pleasure before he took his own climax. It would be a joy to watch Susan cum, and cum again. This was to be no sprint for the finish line. This would be a slow amble through fields of pleasure.

He looked down at her and met her gaze. He saw a softness, a vulnerability in her eyes. She was a delicate flower, to nurture and protect. He loved her. He wanted to please her, be the master she wanted him to be.

Still stroking her hair softly, he kept his voice measured and calm. "Your first act will be one of homage." His free hand unzipped his fly and after a moment of arranging, his penis was fully accessible to her.

Susan gazed at his member. Patrick was pleasingly proportioned. The shaft was thick and the head was nicely rounded. The satin dome of his penis could not conceal a tiny tear of pre-cum. She was close enough for her tongue to slip out and steal the pearl colored liquid. She savored the slightly salty taste, knowing it was only an hors d'oeuvre. She was hungry to consume the next course. She felt the solidness as his big hand cupped the back of her head. She needed no further instruction; she opened her mouth to receive his phallus. He offered it to her slowly and she took the head inside and closed her lips, feeling his warm velvety softness on her tongue. She took no more into her mouth than he had offered, she was content to serve him as he saw fit.

She found his touch soothing and felt comfortable enough to relax even more, surrendering to the moment, enjoying the gentle, soft, feeling of his hand stroking through her hair, as she circled the head of his penis with her tongue.

She loved the caring, nurturing feeling of his fingers softly stroking her hair. It made her feel cherished. For all his dominance, there was no force, nothing aggressive, or hasty. There was as much tenderness and trust in his control as there was power.

Patrick felt her mouth warm and comforting around his

penis. He loved the feeling of being held in that warm wet sanctuary. Although he was highly aroused, he was also in full control. "I would like you to feel the size and shape of my penis."

He looked down seeing her beautiful face turned up toward him. Her lips wrapped around his penis, while her eyes gazed adoringly up at him. The look she gave him made him feel as warm inside as if he'd just downed a cup of hot chocolate. He smiled knowing that with Susan he was at home, regardless of their location.

Still lightly running his fingers through her hair he continued, "You will not speak unless I ask you to speak. When you do speak, I wish you to refer to me as Master or Sir. If at any time something becomes uncomfortable or we need to stop for whatever reason your safe word is red." Patrick withdrew his cock from her mouth and asked, "Is that clearly understood? And are you happy?"

Susan loved that he took so much care with her feelings and took so much time to make sure she was happy. In truth, she was ready for anything, she was so erotically charged. She knew that was the very reason Patrick paid so much attention to these details and she loved him for it. In gratitude, her lips delicately kissed his penis. She would have been happy for him to use her mouth to his climax, and would have gladly satisfied him there, but it was not his will, and not hers to question. It had felt wonderful to have him in her mouth, for as long as he had wanted and she was content to wait for his further instructions. "Yes Sir, I understand. I am happy and waiting to serve you."

Patrick smiled warmly at the lady he loved. He loved that her voice was sweet, clear, and unashamed. "Thank you my pet." He felt a swell of pride in his chest. She had come so far and he delighted that he had been with her on each and every step of her journey to proud submission. He felt it an honor, to call her his. He helped her to her feet. "I wish you to lie on the bed with you hands above your head, please."

Her only reply, as she slid onto the bed was, "Would you like me face up or face down?"

"On your back please my pet." He walked to his briefcase, which he had set by a small table. He stooped and picked up the case, setting it on the table. His fingers nervous with anticipation fiddled with the two small clasps. On pushing two small buttons, there were simultaneous clicks and the spring-loaded locks sprang open.

He took a length of inch thick silk rope and a piece of fabric from the case. He felt the luxurious nap of the fabric as he walked back toward the bed. He had always loved the sumptuous feel of velvet.

Patrick never tired of looking at Susan, gazing at her lovely body. She was a delightful picture lying passively, her arms extended above her head. His eyes roved along her legs, loving the way her hold up stockings looked on her shapely legs. For him it was very erotic to see the way the dark silk clung to her thighs and calves.

He moved to the foot of the bed and lifted her ankle, slipping the shoe from her foot. He played the silk stocking between her toes and massaged her foot. He loved the small cooing and quiet moans she let slip from her lips.

He knew she enjoyed the feel of his hands on her feet, so he lingered. The stockings between her flesh and his hands had a decadent luxurious feel. He was aware of the size and strength of his hands, in comparison to her dainty feet. The nylon slipped between her toes as he manipulated her toes. He felt her splay them, catlike, allowing him to get right between her toes. There was a comfort in his control over her, a comfort that gave a greater meaning to his life. She moaned softly, as he massaged her stockinged feet, her moans and coos of pleasure encouraged him to carry on this firm yet tender massage.

He felt powerful in the giving and was warm in the knowledge that he was the giver of pleasure. He delighted in being the one who had the control and the power to give such pleasure.

Susan sighed, loving the feeling of being pampered. For someone who spent so much of her life on her feet, to have someone do this for her was sheer luxury. She felt the pressure of his hands on her feet. They were warm, strong and powerful. She felt his fingers part her toes, felt his hands as they drifted to her arches, manipulating her pliant flesh. She was putty in his hands. Moans of joy slipped softly from her lips.

The rhythmic massage was in tune with and fuelled by her body's responses. Her muscles squeezed, pulsing with her desire. She felt the two dildos moving inside her, their presence sharpening as her body tightened around them. Ripples built deeply from within, leading slowly to her promised land. The tension started deep within and spiraled out. His hands worked over her arches, squeezing and releasing, a sensation that echoed through the phalluses that penetrated her. Her pelvic floor and vaginal muscles took up the same rhythm of squeezing and releasing. The sensations were taking over and she closed her eyes, as she concentrated on the ever-beating drum of desire. In the darkness of her mind, she was so much more aware of her senses, the heat of her skin, and the ache in her nipples. She arched her back. The movement affected the dildos and she was alive with electric firecrackers of delight.

There was a cascade effect as the intense pleasure of her feet being manipulated rolled together with her double penetration and the anticipation that had been building since the last time they had met. It had all combined and was driving her towards her crisis. She wanted to hold back knowing that her master took a dim view of her cumming without permission. Yet, if she asked, surely he would punish her for talking.

The tension that had been growing larger and larger was close to over-flowing. The feeling seemed to start deep within her with pulsing waves that rippled outward. She bit her lower lip, in a vain attempt to hold back the tide. She moaned uncontrollably as wave after wave washed over her, crest colliding with crest, the physical colliding with the emotional. Her love for Patrick, her never wanting to be away from his side again, wanting him, wanting to be everything for him, wanting to be his slave to do with as he saw fit. The world faded to a haze, the ripples and throbs echoed through her, and she was lost to sensation.

She soared high, hitting the peak. The spasms gripped her, a feeling of tightening, an iron fist gripping, contracting until she hit her crisis point. Then eruption, sensory overload. She felt her body go rigid, pins and needles raked over her, sweet and sour, vinegar over ice water.

Slowly, piece by piece, the world returned. She was panting, small jolts of electric aftershocks, still made her tingle. And there he was, in the aftermath, still massaging her feet.

She found herself, breathless, but beginning to relax. Patrick was stroking her feet. Suddenly, she felt a flush of guilt, as she realized that she had succumbed to an orgasm without permission. She liked the humiliation of having to ask for this most basic of human releases, as she felt it made her service all the more total. She looked up and began to speak. "Sir, I'm sorry that…" her words trailed off with a simple shake of Patrick's head.

Patrick held her foot in his firm grip. He knew her transgression, yet he had very much enjoyed her climax. "My pet, it gave me pleasure to see you cum. It gives me pleasure to give you pleasure." He smiled as he moved along the side of the bed, stroking up her leg as he did so, feeling the silk stockings and loving the sensation. When his hand reached the harness, which was holding the two phalluses in place, he rested his hand on her pubis and softly patted. "But there will be a price to pay. There is always a price to pay."

Susan heard no malice in his voice, only the care of her

loving master. She felt him pat her again on the pubis. She was still sensitive from her climax and her muscles rippled along the two dildos. She found the sensation intensely pleasurable and there was a tremble of pleasure in her voice when she said, "Sir, I am happy to receive any punishment you see fit." The warmth in his smile reassured her that he would never do anything that would ever really hurt her.

Patrick moved further up the bed trailing his fingers across her soft tummy, lingering, languidly stroking, up towards her rounded breasts. He took time fondling each silky breast, stimulating each of her gumdrop nipples to a perfect peak. His velvety voice purred, "Anything I do, I will do for our pleasure." He picked up the piece of velvet he had left on the bed before the foot massage and placed it around her wrists. "I don't want the rope to mark your wrists," he explained as he began to use the rope to secure her hands together. "I may mark you elsewhere, but not where it will show."

His last statement did not disturb Susan. They had played rough games before. He had bound her before. He had never left more than a little bruising that had always faded within a day or so.

Her mind wandered, while his dexterous fingers worked on the rope. She thought of a time when they had played roughly, he had spanked her. She remembered the pleasure in the humiliation of being spanked. They had met up in London while she was on a stop over, covering for a colleague on the European route. To her delight, she had found that Patrick was also in London on business and they were able to spend a glorious night together. It was his expression *'Won't mark you where it shows'* that had triggered this line of thinking, as on that occasion she had gone swimming the next day and the bruises on her ass were still visible.

As she lay there being tied to the headboard, she smiled to herself at the memory of the comments and the eyebrows that had been raised by the sight of the bruises. She had said she had gotten them falling over ice-skating, she could tell nobody believed her; but she hadn't really cared about their suppositions.

Content her hands were secure Patrick surveyed his handiwork. He preferred a single central fixing point as it would allow Susan to be turned. Bondage took a little working out in the beginning to assure safety and to allow accessibility. While looking at Susan he pondered some of his less successful attempts and smiled to himself. He remembered the time he had tied her spread-eagle to the bed in her panties and how it had irked him to cut off the $150 pair.

Patrick prided himself that he had become quite accomplished at the art, and no longer made that kind of mistake. This was confirmed by the lovely lady tied and helpless before him.

He stroked her cheek and down her neck, lingering on her breasts. He loved the feel of her silky soft skin. He cupped her breasts, felt the weight, and grazed her erect nipples with his thumbs.

"My pet, as you know, I like any correction to fit the situation." His eyes met hers as he spoke. She was passive and yet attentive to his words. "Correction should be fun, and any form of learning should be fun too." His hand stroked down her stomach towards the waistband of the harness. His fingers fondled the harness and moved lower to her pubis, where he applied a little pressure.

He heard her moan softly, obviously enjoying the sensation of his hands on her body. He felt the thrill he always felt, when he gave her pleasure. Knowing he had this power over her, it was a benevolent power and wielding it was the greatest aphrodisiac he knew.

He felt his own arousal growing, straining against his tight briefs. A part of him wanted to fuck her right then and there, but the other side of him wanted it to last forever.

Susan felt a need to shut out the rest of the world, to

concentrate on the cascade of sensations and on her master. She closed her eyes, relying on the sensations; she felt his hand, totally in control. He was the one in power, in possession of her, the possession she gave him freely. She wanted to be his. All she wanted to do was serve him, please him, make him happy. She would give him anything he wanted, without reservation; for she knew, her love was safe with him. She trusted him totally, not just with her body but also with her fragile heart.

The hand pressed a little more firmly and the two phalluses moved at his command, the tingling pulse in the very centre of her being slowly grew stronger. The ripples radiated from her core. As he pressed, her pelvic and vaginal muscles contracted. The feelings were so intense she let a little gasp slip out.

"My pet I do this for you, for us." His words focused her, and as he spoke, she listened intently. His hand tapped lightly on her pubis.

She let out a little cry, as she felt the intense pleasure. Her muscles contracted around the two phalluses, simultaneously. The sensation was like a thousand small electric shocks all happening at the same time. She felt a second soft tap and it mimicked the electricity of the first, while at the same time it felt like both dildos had penetrated her more deeply. There was a small gap and in that gap, she mentally begged for the third tap. The pause was excruciating. Then when the third one landed, she prayed the fourth would follow soon. The rhythm of her body's need grew. She found herself raising her hips to meet the pats and as soon as one landed, she was hungry for the next.

The pats became light spanks, the gaps between became smaller. Each soft spank produced a shower of molten sparks. Her mind flashed to a hammer and anvil, each blow of the blacksmith's hammer on the cherry red metal setting off a chain reaction of muscle spasms around the two phalluses. The clench and release of all the interacting sets of muscles, urged her on. She strained upwards aware of the physical presence just above her clit. The spanks to her pubis came at a rhythmic rate and at exactly the right speed. She felt the tension building once more within her, feeling that all too familiar pulse that came from deep within her centre growing stronger and stronger. Her body's grip, grew tighter and tighter. The speed and intensity of the spanks increased, now landing as slaps on her pubis. She heard her own breaths coming in short labored gasps, as muscles clenched and released on the phalluses. The throb of pleasure was insistent, the waves building. She bit her lip trying to control her body's demands. The slaps increased and she felt her control slipping. "Sir may I cum?" She could hear the tension in her voice, a pleading for release.

"For your increased pleasure, and mine, I wish you to hold on. Please." His voice was as smooth and velvety as the fabric around her wrist.

She bit harder on her lip, and tried to concentrate, focusing all her attention on not cumming. She tried to grip the two dildos to stop them moving, not wanting to disappoint her master, wanting to do as he commanded, wanting to hold back the tide that was surely going to crash at any moment.

She struggled desperately to keep control. The sensations became more and more intense the harder she tried to control her body's natural instincts.

"Please Sir?" There was no mistaking the strain in her voice. It was hard, yet she wanted to please her master, and she wanted to hold on. She felt the waves breaking on the shores of her desire and knew she was approaching the promised land. "Sir?" It was almost a squeak.

Each spank warmed his hand further, as he shared her physical sensations. He remembered the late nights on the phone, recalled the same strain in her voice, the sounds she made when she wanted to cum, the same sounds she made in the flesh. He looked down and saw the contorted lines on her face. He could not mistake the tension she felt. It was clear in the tone of pleading in her voice. He could tell just how close she was, right on the cusp.

In a way he felt mean, denying her the thing she wanted most right now. In truth, he would have liked to have said yes upon her first request, but he knew by stretching her, the orgasm that she finally got, would be more intense and sweeter for the wait. The denial was the same for him. He had wanted to consume her as soon as he laid eyes on her in the café and his nagging erection had been urging him to do just that, at every opportunity, yet he denied himself the immediate gratification in favor of a longer more pleasurable time together.

He wanted her to hold back for as long as possible, yet he knew, by the strain in her voice, that the fruit was ripe for the picking. "You may cum now my pet."

He continued to spank her pubis, generally lighter, but more varied, from spanks to taps, they landed one after another and at a slightly slower rate. Patrick tried to gage how the spanks affected her, assessing the pleasure of each strike. He watched as her orgasm took her, each flinch and twitch a contraction. Her face contorted as the orgasm swept over her, wave after wave showed on her face and in each twitch of her body. He loved that he was the one who had taken her to this point, that he was the source of her pleasure and her release. Her bliss showed in every line on her face, the way she tilted her head back, jaw line tight, body rigid, toes pointed. He thought it a privilege to be right there, the instigator of her ecstasy, enjoying her rapture.

"Thank…you…Sir." Her voice trembled, her words tumbling out, coming in thick gasps.

Her voice made him feel strong and at the same time, so wanted, so needed.

Patrick watched her prone form, joyously sharing the aftershocks of her climax.

Looking down at his love, he felt in control, every bit the

dominant that they both wanted him to be. His hand now still, applied a little pressure to her pubis, feeling every little tremor, each tiny pulse, which reverberated through her.

He could hear that her breathing was becoming less labored as aftershocks began to fade. He enjoyed the feeling of her winding down, comparing, in his own mind, the contrast between Susan calming down and his erection's persistent demands. Yet despite his own hunger and need, he wanted to remain focused on Susan. He wanted her and he was going to have her, totally and completely, but all in good time.

Patrick felt it was his self-restraint that gave him control. It was his willpower that would take them both to the heights of ecstasy. He knew when he did finally have her, he wanted to make love to every part of her. He loved her with every part of his being and was going to make her totally his.

Allowing her a minute's respite, he stepped back to give her a little space. As he looked down at her, he saw the rapture on her face. He felt a sense of deep fulfillment, to be the one who gave so much pleasure. It was for him more satisfying than his own release.

As he undid his cuffs, he looked down on her and asked, "Can I get you a drink?"

She smiled and slowly shook her head, a look of exhausted, contentment on her face.

He thought she looked radiantly beautiful in her post-orgasmic afterglow. His fingers moved to his shirt buttons flicking them open one by one. Once they were all open, he pulled his shirt from his trousers.

Susan felt spaced out and a bit fuzzy around the edges. She heard his words, yet was happy to lay still and slowly shake her head. There was a dreamlike quality to her experiences. She tingled all over. She felt wonderfully mellow, as she basked in the heat of her own orgasm, while watching the man she loved stripping for her. She enjoyed the sight of him removing his shirt. Her breathing was still heavy, but it was gradually slowing. She watched her breasts rise and fall with her breaths, noticed her erect nipples, and the sheen of perspiration that covered the blush of pink skin on her chest. She did feel hot, but it was a glorious warmth.

With little ceremony Patrick threw his shirt on the chair, he had placed his waistcoat on earlier. He kicked off his shoes and tapped them under the same chair, and then his socks. She loved his casual, self-confident manner as she watched him over her rising and falling chest, finding herself mesmerized by his presence before her. She watched fascinated, as he unfastened his belt and undid the catch on the front of his pants. There was strength in his hands, as he removed his pants. Although his hands were physically powerful they were dexterous, a duality of power and control. His trousers slipped smoothly down his hips pooling at his feet. He stooped to pick them up, folding them so the creases were together and then neatly placed them on the back of the chair on top of the vest. He stood there for a moment. Their eyes met. She wondered what was going through his mind as he looked at her. She hoped that he could see how much she wanted him. His smile told her that he wanted her and the straining bulge against his briefs told her that his body craved her.

They kept eye contact, as Patrick thumbed down his briefs and tossed them casually onto the chair. She watched him return to the bed his penis standing prominently before him. She licked her lips in anticipation of feeling the hard member inside her, his weight on her. His hands unclasped the harness, which held the dildos in place. His hands removed the belt slowly and eased out the two phalluses.

She let slip a little "oooooh" as the first slipped from her vagina. She felt him pause for a moment. She closed her eyes, as his fingers took hold of the second. It had been in place for some time now and as she felt him ease it from her, her lips pursed a little and she sucked in a little air. The phallus slipped from her. A dull ache replaced the fullness she had felt, but that ache was in her master's service and was a small price for the pleasure she had received.

She expected him to mount her either from the front or to turn her and take her from behind, but she was delighted when he parted her legs and took a position between her thighs to pleasure her with his mouth.

Patrick feasted. He had always enjoyed being the giver of pleasure and he had always enjoyed oral sex as giver, as well as recipient. His tongue explored her beautiful petals, finding joy as the tip of his tongue played in all the joyous folds. He was engrossed in his task, but he could hear Susan's appreciative moans. He heard a little grunt of satisfaction as his tongue traveled from the hooded pearl to the glistening opening, neglecting nothing on the journey. He dipped his tongue inside her velvet box, lapping as a kitten at her nectar. He felt her hips lift upward. Feeling she needed more his fingers slipped to her pubis, still red from its recent attention. Dexterous fingers carefully drew the hood from the pearl and softly stroked the hood while his tongue played.

Susan made little whimpering noises. He found he loved the soundscape every bit as much as he enjoyed the taste and scent of his lover. He wanted to please her. Her soft melodic moans were music to his ears, spurring him on, urging him to play his tongue deeper. His mouth wet with her nectar he took her with his mouth. As he thrust his tongue deep, she moaned and pushed up to meet him. He applied a little pressure to her clit and she moaned again. He sensed that she was close to climax. He knew her body well, knew the telltale signs; the way her breath came in short gasps, let out in little mewing whimpering noises, the way her body tensed beneath his touch. She was so responsive. It felt like he was playing an erotic sexual instrument.

His eyes flicked up to see Susan's teeth gripping her lower lip and her hands strained against her bonds. He slipped his tongue from the depths of her pussy to lick along her inner lips, letting his tongue dance on her labia, before plunging it deep into her once more. His face was wet with her nectar, as he used his tongue to fuck her wantonly open pussy. Slipping again from within her, he returned to the soft moist folds. As he took her inner labia in his mouth, he felt the hot wetness of her soft skin. He could feel the tension coiled within her as he sucked and played with her lips with his tongue. Susan responded with a more insistent moan.

She closed her eyes surrendering to sensations. Her other senses seemed to be enhanced by the deprivation of sight. Her nose caught the scents of her own sex mingled with his aftershave. In her heightened state, she could smell wafts of scent, as if carried on a gentle wind from the tropics. She felt his breath against her wet flesh. She listened intently to the slurping, sucking sounds picturing in her minds eye what he was doing with his mouth and tongue to create the sensations she felt. Her heart thumped in her chest, she felt the bonds against her wrists and her whole body tensed, sweet and sour ripples of passion building.

Patrick felt the storm brewing. The waves lapping at the shore had intensified. He sensed whitewater as the odd wave turned into a rolling ball of spume. He knew sensations and emotions became entwined, the edges blurred as the waves rolled over her. He could see in her facial contortions the turmoil that surrounded her. He felt the deep pulse in her clit and imagined how she would abandon herself to the coming crisis. He urged her on wanting her to go over the edge, for her pleasure and for his own.

Susan felt the pulsing grip on her, "P-p Please Sir?" her voice trembled. She was lost in the feelings as the breakers strummed and whirled around her nub of pleasure. She clamped down harder on her lip to try to hold back the thrashing tide that was bringing her to her orgasm.

She heard Patrick give a small grunt, as he continued his ministrations of lust, at her altar of Venus. If it was a yes or no, she was not certain, but at that point, she could not have stopped herself. The approaching climax was like a feral beast that nipped at her threatening to ravage her. Then it had her, overpowering her.

Pants and gasps poured from her, the concentration and power surprised her, overwhelmed her. She could not differentiate what was happening. It was a jumble of reality and emotion, a kaleidoscope of sensation, the feeling of wetness, melting, and all the while the squeeze and release of her muscles. Tingling waves, and all the time the insistent throbbing. She felt her thighs lock, clamping around his head locking him securely to her. She needed total stillness as her body went rigid. The spasms gripped her. A cry passed her lips. It was as if a swirl of lights buzzed around her head. She was warm and tingly, sweet and sour, sugar and vinegar. Joy.

The warmth and joy spread over her as wave after wave washed over her, overlapping, cascading, tumbling, gripping in contraction on top of contraction. Time and space had no meaning. The sensations could have lasted a minute or an hour.

The next thing that she was aware of for sure was the release of tension and Patrick's presence. He was softly stroking her thigh. His hand was warm and soothing. She felt like an adored pet, and she loved the feeling. It was like being wrapped in cotton wool, warm, and safe. She felt totally relaxed, sated from the depth of release. She felt cared for and cherished.

She loved Patrick and the way he gave so freely and selflessly. She would do anything to give him the same level of satisfaction that he gave her. She looked down and caught him gazing back up at her. She smiled, happy to give herself completely to him.

Patrick felt elated. He enjoyed giving her pleasure and to see her laying there panting after her third orgasm gave him immense pleasure. To give so much felt empowering.

He knew it was drawing close to the time when he had to

consider his own needs. He kissed her inner thigh and pulled back rising from the bed. He feasted his eyes on his beautiful Susan; she was all he would ever want. She was radiant, her skin glistening with a pink flush across her cheek and chest. He smiled as he looked down at her, knowing he had to have her. The sight of her tied hands aroused him even more. That she was tied and defenseless roused the caveman that lived deep inside him, making him want to devour her.

He stroked his aching penis, and felt his tight shaven balls. His hunger had become ravenous.

He looked down at Susan. Though her arms were tied above her head, she laid languidly, her legs unashamedly apart and he could see her vermillion tinted labia lips glistening with desire. He looked up into her eyes and saw the same smoldering desire; she returned a wonderfully passive *'I'm yours for the taking'* smile. He placed his hands on her thighs. Her skin was hot to the touch. She made neither comment nor protest, as he parted her legs further.

Susan loved the feeling of helplessness, of being laid open, on the sacrificial altar. She was such a willing sacrifice.

She felt the mattress move, as he climbed onto the bed. There was something of the predator about him, stalking his prey, rather than going in for the kill. She felt his hands on her feeling her breasts, lightly squeezing, kneading. Hands lingered, stroking her, moving down her sides to her stomach. Down further to her pubis, as he touched her she still felt small aftershocks from her last climax. She was aware of his weight as he loomed over her.

He was silent, a bird of prey about to swoop. She reveled in the act of being taken, the closeness of him, his mass, his masculine scent enveloping her, the weight of his body, as he knelt between her legs. Her fantasies ran riot in her mind. She imagined herself the slave girl about to be ravaged by her master. And there she was fantasy come true, tied, helpless, open, and ready for him. She felt him enter her. Sliding his long dagger smoothly and in a single motion into her velvet lined sheath.

She knew that she had the power to stop him with a word, if she wished, but she didn't. She wanted to be ravaged, as they had acted out so many times before. She'd had fantasies about being taken, roughly, by a tall, dark, and handsome stranger. She knew that this image turned Patrick on too and she wanted to make this good for him.

She closed her eyes tight and pictured her lover, as that stranger, silent but for animal like grunts, as he thrust between her velvet folds. His hardness, pounded mercilessly into her soft yielding body. Knowing the act of him fucking her hard, didn't match the violence of the fantasy in her mind didn't matter. His hard body pressed her to the bed and she used her muscles to grip him tightly, wanting to please him. She loved the meld of fantasy and reality.

The fantasy playing out in her mind had him taking her cruelly, raping innocent flesh. She felt his hips thrust, grinding into her, the lines between fantasy and reality hazy, as his balls slapped hard against her bottom while one hand gripped her breast and the other gripped her hair.

Her mind played out the fantasy scene in vividly colored pictures, her running blindly through the night, her assailant panting for breath as he chased her, her violent capture, then being tied, forced to the bed and being ravished. In her mind it was a violent act, her body raped. But there was the irony; this was a joyful act, a willing rape, a fantasy.

She knew he would never be party to an un-consensual act. Yet the fantasy fuelled her desire. Her heart raced as her body began the build up to another crisis. The rhythm beat in her chest. She felt his thrusts, felt his pubis grinding against her own. In approaching her own crisis, she wanted to give her lover as much pleasure as he gave her. She felt her body becoming very tightly focused, as the grip of spasms took hold. Her toes curled and her body went tense, as she rode the crest of the wave. The world became less than solid, as time went into free fall.

The next thing she was aware of was him, still on top of her, still inside her. His pace had slowed. She could feel every last inch of his hard cock as he used its full length, slipping from her, then plunging to her very depths. Her body still twitched from her climax, the long slow penetration held her close to the edge of another orgasm.

There was a slow rise and fall as his cock stretched her. It felt like he was reaming her, yet it was a lovely sensation. Her contracting vaginal muscles clenched around his rigid cock, as he took her long and slow. Her orgasm was protracted, lingering for as long as he kept moving. Suddenly a wave of guilt passed through her. Had her master cum? She didn't know. Her own throes of passion had clouded her mind.

He felt it to be a natural break and slowed his pelvic thrusts, to a stop. He felt her muscles rhythmically gripped around his manhood. They lay still together for a time, his weight on her, fixing her to the bed. He basked in the warm feeling of Susan's contentment, lingering in the afterglow of her receding orgasm.

She felt Patrick take his weight on his arms, as he slipped from her. She let out a slight whimper, feeling the loss. She missed the feeling of his member inside her. He lifted himself up and rolled onto his side, cuddling into her.

Patrick kissed her lightly on her shoulder, "How do you feel, my pet?"

She looked into his eyes, a deep sense of satisfaction filling her heart, "I feel wonderful, Sir truly wonderful." she paused, not really knowing if she should talk or not. "May I ask a question Sir?"

She felt his warm lips on her shoulder as he kissed her. "Of course my Pet."

Susan hesitated, almost embarrassed to ask the question. She felt wet, but she had been so absorbed with her own climax, she was not sure if Patrick had reached his. "Please Sir, have you cum?" She felt silly asking, but she wanted to know, she wanted to know if he'd had as much pleasure, as she had. She wanted so badly to please him. She held her breath for the answer.

He kissed her and fondled her breast. "My pet, I have been saving myself. No I have not cum yet, my choice not to." He kissed her shoulder again. "I want to savor you; I plan to cum deep within you soon. It has been such a long time and I wanted to take my time, and enjoy you. I have enjoyed you and I intend to go on enjoying you, my pet"

Chapter Five

Time for the Encore

She felt replete from their lovemaking, held tightly by the man she loved, his words of devotion fresh in her ears. In Patrick's arms, she felt so safe, so right. He made her feel cherished, adored.

She loved his silent closeness, the warmth of his body pressed to her, still, but for his finger slowly tracing abstract patterns on her arm. They lay spoon-like on the bed skin to naked skin. His body hard and strong, she felt his powerful bicep, as he held her soft, yielding body tightly. This intimate, loving, respite felt soft after the passionate lovemaking.

Patrick loved the feel of her soft skin against his body in this quiet tender moment. Lying there, his mind considered the possibilities of their future together, daydreaming of a time when they would never be parted. His mind weighed the balance of pros and cons of how it would work. There would be less money that was true, but being together was worth more than money. Would it work on a full time basis? Would it be something Susan would want? Could they actually live together? They got on so well, surely it was silly to think like that.

All the while he thought the watches ticked away their

remaining moments of time together.

Time was always the thing, fleeting moments together were no longer enough. There was a limit to how long he could cope with the times they were apart. He knew he wanted to wake up with this lady every day of his life. He kissed her shoulder and ran his fingers through her silky soft hair.

This quiet moment allowed him to watch her quietly, aware of her breathing, enjoying his voyeuristic view of her breasts, as her chest rose and sank slowly with each breath. Her skin was smooth and moving softly, to the rhythm of her breathing. His hand on her skin felt no sign of any tension in her body. She looked perfectly relaxed, the wisp of a smile on her lips showed her happy state of mind and he shared her sunny disposition.

Looking at Susan's prone form, and the feel of her peachy flesh, began to revive thoughts of carnal pleasure. His mind conjured up images of his love serving him constantly and his penis twitched into life. The more he thought of Susan in his service, the more ardent his erection became. His grip on her tightened as he pressed into her, hugging her warm body to his. He felt the pressure of his erect penis, as it pressed against her thigh.

He never wanted to be parted from her, how this felt here and now, was just so right.

He stroked his hand, from her hair to her neck, lightly brushing the skin from her earlobe to her collarbone, loving the slight moaning noise, she made. He lingered in the places that produced the lowest throaty sounds, teasing the moans from her lips. His fingers drifted down her arm and across to her breast. The skin responded to his touch, stiffening into two tight gumdrops. As he softly squeezed the hard flesh, his penis twitched against her thigh and his mind drifted to carnal thoughts. Feeling his erection's call, his hand drifted south. Her tummy was soft, and very flat. His finger rimmed around her navel before drifting to her pubis, soft and cleanly shaven, the way he loved it. She moaned softly as his finger dipped into the moistened cleft. He lingered and loved the cooing noise she made as he played with her.

Patrick's yearning to take her grew stronger, and the battle within started again. Whether to take her in an animal like way or whether to consume her slowly like a delicate fruit, this conflict was always with him. He knew his self-control would win over the animal, but the animal was always there.

His fingers slowly played with her moist clit, while he studied her. She was radiant with the pink glow of a woman that had been freshly fucked and was ready to be fucked again. Patrick kissed her and said, "My pet I am hungry for you, are you ready to serve again?"

Her smile was warm enough to melt snow, and in her smile, he could see her willingness to serve, "Yes Master. Do with me as you will. I am all yours."

Patrick felt his heart pound in his chest. He sucked cool air into his hot throat. Her words lifted him high and made him feel strong and wanted. He felt his penis throb. He wanted her more than ever before.

He wanted her physically, yes, but even more than that, he wanted her because she was the part that made him whole and he never wanted that feeling to go away. He wanted this feeling to last forever.

He moved back slightly to give himself some room and taking her leg, he turned her onto her stomach. She helped as much as she could, as he lifted her hips and slipped a pillow under them. He did his best to make her position more comfortable for her and more agreeable to him. He saw her steal a glance over her shoulder, giving him an appreciative smile, as he made her comfortable. He felt her wiggle just a little, as he stroked the soft peachy skin of her bottom. He kissed her ass cheek softly. She moaned pushing back, as if offering him her body. He enjoyed her wantonness. He kissed her again harder this time taking in the view of her smooth derrière.

His nimble fingers removed the dildo from the harness that she had worn earlier, and after kissing the tip, he slipped the phallus into her expectant pussy. Her sigh reassured him that it was a welcome guest. Patrick bent and kissed the cheek of her bottom again lingering longer than he had the first time. He felt her push back a little lifting her bottom to him, and cooing softly.

"I need you my pet," Patrick whispered softly in her ear.

Susan cooed and wiggled her bottom playfully. "I am yours for the taking." She knew and shared his tastes. She loved the power exchange inherent in anal sex. It made her feel so submissive.

From the very first time he had taken her there, it had felt so right. She had worried beforehand. She had read a lot of negative things in women's magazines and she was worried about the pain everyone talked about.

Looking back on her first time, what she remembered most was the care and consideration he had shown her. She had been nervous as he was preparing her. She remembered that he had used a lot of lube and had taken a long time fingering her and opening her. She loved that he gave her time to become accustomed to the new sensations. When the time had come there was a little discomfort, but no pain, just a little ache as she got used to his member inside her. After that, there had been an intense feeling of well-being.

She felt so compliant to receive him in that way and she loved the way her compliance made her feel. In a way, it made her feel naughty, but feeling naughty with the man you love and trust, she considered a beautiful thing. When she had felt him possess her delicate niche, she had felt special. She was his, owned, in a very fundamental way. There was something profoundly submissive about being buggered. It was so controlled and the level of trust she gave him so deep, way beyond what she had given any other lover.

She felt Patrick's finger, softly stroke her precious rose bud. He leaned over her back and whispered, "You know what I would like, it would please me if you ask." He had always liked her to ask. Using sexual language had never come naturally to her; in fact, it had taken her quite a while to be able to talk in a sexually graphic way. Patrick had been patient and encouraging using baby steps to desensitize her.

She knew from all their conversations on the subject of sex that there were two good reasons for her to vocalize the request. She knew that he needed to feel that the act was truly consensual and that he felt that if she asked she must really want this intimate act to happen, as much as he did. She also knew that he loved the power he felt when he heard her ask. She remembered that he had said how much he loved the slight humiliation of her having to ask, and though she had never told him, she enjoyed it too.

There was a naughtiness, something about her sweet innocent voice asking to be buggered, and she knew by his state of arousal, that he found the words an immense turn on. Knowing it aroused him so much, made it exciting for her to talk dirty for him.

He remembered when they had first become intimate, how hard it had been for him to get Susan to speak aloud about her erotic thoughts and ideas. She had really found it difficult. He knew her mother's *"nice girls don't say that, nice girls don't do that"* rang in here ears. And she was a nice girl.

Patrick had started her off slowly word-by-word, starting with medical terms for his and her genitals. She knew the words, but it felt unnatural to her to speak them aloud.

During many long nights spent chatting on the phone, he had introduced her to the joy of possessing words, starting with the medical text book words for their genitals, which didn't seem so bad, as it was the kind of thing she might have to say on a doctor's visit. Then in stages, he introduced slang terms, and unusual ethnic words from such texts as the Kama Sutra. Patrick had painstakingly helped her step-by-step, over each barricade her mother had worked so hard to build. It had been a long process, but she had seen the daylight, though he knew she still thrilled to the naughty element of it.

Susan admired Patrick's eclectic knowledge of the language of eroticism. It was not that she had never heard the words before, or that she hadn't used them in her head, or as profanities on the odd occasion. It was context, using the words to vocalize her desires that had felt odd at first.

Patrick asking her to do this for him was another way of him exercising his control over her and she liked that aspect too. Over time, it had become easier and once she had found her erotic voice, she realized and delighted in the feeling of power it gave her. She remembered Patrick confessing to her one night on the phone, that she had gotten him to the brink of climax with a few erotic words. She found that knowledge a turn on. It was empowering to have that much power over another. It was then she had understood the intoxication of power exchange, to be the one who bestowed pleasure.

Susan's body tingled now, knowing the affect her words would have on him. It was with relish she said slowly and clearly, "Please Sir, would you do me the honor, of sodomizing me?" Even now, her words sounded wonderfully naughty, as they tripped from her lips.

For Patrick anal sex was the antithesis of domination and submission in the trust it took from the receiver and the power it gave to the giver. Just Susan speaking the words describing the act, sodomy and buggery, could give him an erection.

Delight at her ease in expressing her desires surged through him filling his chest with pride. She had been so timid, it had taken many hours to get her here, but the confidence in her voice now made him proud. Her words, freely spoken, gave him the power.

She had always said she wanted him to be her master, and he wanted to be the man who loved and possessed her.

"Thank you my pet, it would give me enormous pleasure." That simple sentence made him feel exuberant with the power she had given him. He wanted her.

Applying a little lube to his finger, he slipped a digit into her delightfully tight anus. She moaned softly. It was a glorious sound, sweet music to his ears.

His finger slipped in easily, the earlier penetration of the dildo having already relaxed her and she took the second finger easily too. She pushed back, with a soft exhalation of breath.

Patrick heard his own growl of desire vibrating in his throat. The beast was close to the surface, but still on the leash. As much as the beast pulled at the tether he knew he must prepare the way thoroughly. He had taken her this way many times before, yet he never took this tender opening for granted. He always made sure she was ready for him. He had no wish to abuse such a delicate flower.

She moaned softly and he felt her push back against his fingers, obviously feeling comfortable and wanting more. A third finger entered her smoothly and he knew she was ready.

He smeared more lube on his swollen cock and offered the head to her dilated portal. The merest pressure and the spear point entered. She let out the smallest whimper, as he applied a little pressure.

Her anus was hot and slippery. He felt the pressure on his penis as he stretched her, delighting in her pleasure as her moan grew louder. He heard her exhale as he reached the tightest part. He gave her a moment to become accustomed to the sensation. When he felt she was ready, he pressed a little more and rather than shy away, he felt Susan pushing back, letting out short gasps of breath as she did. The sensation around his cock was intense. His heart pounded. Elation swept through him. He pressed a little more and his cock was buried to the zenith of the helmets girth. Then there was a pop as it passed the crisis point and the ring of muscle tightened on his shaft. He allowed her, as he always had, the time to relax and get used to him there. He wanted her ready, yet his balls were tight and ached for release.

The beast raised an eyebrow.

He waited, giving her the power to push back, rather than him pushing further. He had not more than a moment to wait before Susan gave a little moan, moved back and the head of his penis disappeared into her bottom.

Groaning with the pleasurable sensation of her body admitting then closing tightly around his cock, he slowly eased inside, wanting to savor the penetration himself and knowing that Susan also enjoyed this slow domination. Millimeter by millimeter he entered her; his sighs and gasps matching hers as slowly, yet painlessly he entered her fully. He leaned over her back and kissed her neck. "Good girl," he whispered in her ear.

Between short easy, open-mouthed breaths, she whispered back, "Thank you."

He granted her a moment to become accustomed to the sensation of being filled. He heard her coo softly, and felt her anal muscle ripple around his penis. In this quiet moment, he delighted in the naughtiness of the act, still illegal between men and women in some countries. The sensation was intense, the tight grip around his shaft making him feel connected to Susan not just physically but spiritually too. He felt her move and the muscles rippled around his shaft. They had often talked about whether the contractions of those muscles alone would be enough to make him cum. He had no doubt now that they would be. But that would be for another time.

He started a small rocking motion, a matter of a centimeter or so at first, each rock taking him a little deeper. The rocking continued, deeper and deeper, taking her completely until he was buried to the hilt. Susan let out a satisfied "oooh!" He paused briefly and then started the rocking motion again. The strokes built up slowly, less than an inch to start with, a gentle motion, in and out. His strokes became longer, and he felt the ripples of muscles as he slowly fucked her. He wanted her to feel the full length of his cock. He wanted to possess her totally, to be her master. His cock slid slowly the full length of her back passage the head slipping from her and entering her anew each time. Her moans of pleasure urged him on. The tight passage squeezed his cock and the sensation was intense. He knew Susan wanted it to be good for both of them and he loved that she gave and she also received.

The beast growled.

His thrusts became a little more ardent. Susan's gasps became a little louder and a little closer together. The sounds of her pleasure fuelled his passion. She was pinned to the bed his stomach molded to her bottom. Hot, fevered, sweat dripped from his forehead onto her back as he pumped into her. He fucked her full tilt now, the strokes shorter and much faster in that hot, tight passage. Intermingled with her cries of pleasure, he heard his balls slapping against her wet pussy lips, as he drove ever closer to his climax.

He slackened the leash on the beast as he felt his crisis building ever higher. He knew he would not last long, but was determined to last as long as he could. Patrick gritted his teeth. He needed Susan to cum with him. It was never enough to cum on his own. He needed to give, not only his cum but he needed to give Susan her own release.

His body bent over her back, he moved one hand to the delicate nub of her clit. The other curled around to cup her breast, his finger and thumb teasing and softly squeezing her nipple. He pinned her to the bed, his throaty growl in harmony with her moans of ecstasy. He was determined to bring her to a climax with him, determined that they get to that promised land together. Her cries became more urgent, as did his. The spasms were on him and he felt her ass muscles gripping at his cock, as he thrust into her.

She was so close, she felt as if she was floating, tingling, it was a series of overwhelming sensations. She felt the pressure of his fingers on her clit and nipple, his hard chest pressed into her back, his hips thrusting, bouncing off her ass. She felt his heat, his power as he covered her. Her heart raced feeling his need, as surely as she felt her own.

She heard his grunts as he pounded into her, together with his monosyllabic chant of *"Fuck yeah! Fuck yeah!"* The chant added fuel to the already rich tapestry of erotic imagery, which filled her head, as he rode her tight back passage. Her mind was filled with the sensations of hard cock, wet pussy, tight ass and stiff clit. She felt taken, possessed, wanted. Every nerve ending beat with the rhythm of her heart, racing full pelt for oblivion. In the tousled mêlée, she heard his voice whisper in her ear, "Cum, cum now for me my pet."

There were stars, a total overload of sensations. She was oblivious to all around her, as a million sparks exploded within her, as the world was lost in soft focus.

His crisis was building to an imminent crescendo. He bucked faster and faster. He was vaguely aware of his grip on her nipple and clit, but things were becoming unclear as to what was happening and what was in his mind. The cave man stirred inside him. In his mind, hard images of hard cocks, plowing tight asses, were pushing him towards the precipice. His grunts turned to a growl and his *"Fuck yeah! Fuck yeah!"* chant became less coherent. He felt the contractions of her ass grab his cock with a vice like grip. He pushed deep, as deep as he could, growling, *"Take it! Take it! Take it! Take it!"* Then he held himself still, his climax washing over him in jerky spasm after spasm. His mind filed with a myriad of mental images, a tortes-like outpouring of cock and cum, of tight ass and hot cunt. The sweet and sour. The clench of her tight muscles. Her spasms. Her orgasm. With a throaty moan and short gasps of breath, he bit his lip and strained, as he spilled his very essence deep within her. He felt rush after rush, from his cock and the warm wetness of his liquid gift to her.

All was quiet. Time had no dominion.

Slowly the world came back into focus. The only thing he was aware of at first was the thumping of his own heart and Susan's tight muscular spasms around his cock. Then he became aware of his own gasps of air onto the back of her neck.

He heard Susan's pants for breath. "Sweetie, are you ok?"

She nodded and in a hoarse voice, whispered, "Fine."

Patrick looked around. Their bodies glistened, bathed in a fine sweat. He relaxed, more than content to stay where he was. He was spent, totally drained of any energy and at peace with the world. Occasionally, he felt his penis involuntarily twitch; his member seemed to have a life of its own. He was still inside Susan, but she seemed content for him to stay there. She made small contented noises, as someone replete after a large meal.

Coming round a little more, seeing Susan's hands still tied to the bed, he reached up and slackened the tethers freeing her arms and massaging, what he guessed would be aching flesh. She responded with a series of cat-like sighs.

Susan had been transported by their passion, to a place of ecstasy. They lay exhausted in each other's arms, his chest pressed into her back, his muscular thighs pressed up against her buttocks. She loved the cocooned feeling of Patrick's strong arms wrapped around her. She felt warm and cherished with his hot naked skin pressed tightly against her. She felt him stir as he cuddled into her, his hands cupping her breasts. She covered his hands with her own, as his fingers delicately played with her tender nipples.

Her body tingled. The feeling was a little like floating on a cloud or waking first thing in the morning and not knowing where dreams had stopped and reality had started. And like waking from a dream, reality began to intrude. She was aware of his slowly softening member still inside her.

He softly kissed the peach fuzz on the nape of her neck, letting his lips catch on her skin. Then he lightly blew on the moistened flesh, seeming to delight in the goose flesh that puckered up and her minuscule shudder.

Patrick tightened his grip on her and pulled her back tight against him, preventing his cock from slipping out. He enjoyed the feel of her body so soft and smooth and he stroked her, from her shoulders down her side, from waist to hip, down her smooth round thigh, lingering, enjoying the feel of her silky skin, before slowly migrating back up to fondle her breasts.

He felt drained by the exertion of the last few hours, but fought his body's urge to fall asleep with the desire to be with the lady he loved, to drink in every sensation. He was aware that his penis was losing its strength and although it was still inside that tight dark portal, he was a little disappointed, when he felt it start to slip.

He kissed her ear tenderly and whispered, "Are you ok? Did I hurt you?"

Susan felt relaxed. She loved the concern he showed her, after the passion they had shared. She looked over her shoulder and smiled "I feel wonderful." His body still covered hers, but the grip was lessening now, as she felt his penis slip out to nestle between her cheeks like a sleepy snail.

He was aware of the lethargy of his subsiding erection and kissed the back of her neck, as he slipped from her cleft. Patrick rolled onto his back and carefully guided Susan to follow the roll, so she ended up with her face on his chest looking up into his eyes. Her adoring gaze made him feel immensely wanted. It made him feel that he was the Master she wanted him to be. Her love for him shone through and was echoed in his own heart. He loved this lady with all his heart and the look she gave him, proved to him that she loved him with the same generous abandon. He broke the magic spell by saying, "I wish we could stay like this forever," as his hand strolled through her hair.

His words had obviously echoed her thoughts. "That would be wonderful. I want nothing more than that," she said, nuzzling her cheek into his chest, her smile telling him that she was enjoying the feeling of his hand stroking her hair.

"Maybe it is time to end our nomadic lifestyle and settle down a bit." Patrick paused, thinking of the ramifications of that statement. A desk bound job would not have the status as his current job, nor the financial dividends. Yet how much of that mattered really? He loved the feel of her hair, as the thin gossamer strands slipped between his fingers. He contemplated all the things he hated about his job, the hours at airports, all made more laborious with the advent of heightened security. It was living out of suitcases and never feeling he was really home. He looked down at Susan. The good parts of his job seemed nothing compared to her love and devotion. Surely a real home with Susan would be a dream come true. Any sacrifices made would be more than worth it.

Susan looked up into his eyes. For a long time she had wanted to lead a more normal life, but every time she thought of the word normal, the word *boring* popped into her mind, but looking at Patrick laid back, looking so relaxed, she saw that normal didn't have to be boring. She smiled and kissed his chest. Another thought popped into her mind, it was something she had considered many times, but had dismissed as hoping too much, but this visit had given her the courage to dare to dream this could go all the way, that this time he would actually propose. And if he did, what would she say? *God I hope he proposes.*

Patrick continued to stroke her hair "Remember when we got the watches from that old guy Zachariah?" he paused, looking for the right words. He so wanted this to sound right.

In reply, Susan nodded remembering with delight, the encounter in the seedy part of town. She felt a tension in the air as if something big was about to happen and oh god she hoped it was the answer to her dreams.

Patrick continued, "I was thinking I would like to go back

to The Crimson Z and fulfill our bargain with the jeweler." He paused momentarily, again getting it right in his ear. It was what he wanted and he hoped she would say yes. "Susan… Will you marry me?" He felt his heart pounding, as he said the words. He felt euphoric, yet there was a tiny twinge of apprehension.

Susan's heart soared to the heavens. Everything she had hoped for. Her heart pounded in her chest, as she whispered the word, a pure and simple, "Yes."

They embraced holding each other, both knowing this was right. He knew that Susan was the one he wanted to spend his life with. He loved the feel of her body so close to him, but it was more than her body, she was his soul mate, his partner in the joyous dance of life, and he wanted this dance to go on forever.

Chapter Six

The Times to Come

They lay there for what seemed like hours kissing and cuddling, fondling each other softly, gently, in a way that would not lead to anything more than just enjoying each other's bodies and their closeness, content in their nakedness.

A wild thought fluttered into his mind. He knew that going back to The Crimson Z, was right, yet the loan of the powers Zachariah had bestowed on them would be a hard thing to give up. The power to stop time was exciting, oh so very useful and above all so unbelievably fun to use. He looked at the two watches on the bedside table, both said 1:30, exactly the same time that they had read when he had put them together.

Patrick had always been a have your cake and eat it too kind of a guy. "I wonder if we didn't go back, I mean just kept the watches as they are..." As soon as the words passed his lips, he hated himself for saying them. He had always been honest, and had never reneged on a deal. He knew this was no time to start. It was testimony to the potency of the power that he had even considered it.

He glanced at Susan. She had an expression on her face, like a puppy that has just had its tail stepped on. He could see from the expression in her eyes, that she was a little disappointed in him.

He felt a little ashamed at even contemplating backtracking on the agreement. "No, I was being silly. We will go back to Zachariah. He will make the rings. We have had our fun with the watches."

Susan smiled up at him. She was happy he had only slipped from the pedestal she had put him on for one brief moment. She traced a finger over his chest and kissed his nipple. "Yes we have had fun, I have loved every moment. And I will go on loving every moment we are together." She kissed his nipple again and looked up into his adoring eyes.

There was a comfortable lull. Patrick continued to stroke her hair and she snuggled into his chest. The pleasant silence stretched without need for words. The moment one that only two people that were totally at ease with each other could share.

Susan broke the silence. She let out a sweet little chuckle as she recalled, "Remember the time we used the watches on the plane when we were flying to Seattle?"

"Will I ever forget? It was the night we joined the mile high club. There isn't a lot of room for maneuver in those bathrooms." There was a snicker in his voice. "Damn good fun though." He paused and then recalled, "There was that time in the departure lounge rest room."

Susan moved up the bed a little and kissed his shoulder. "You stole my panties, before take off and I had to spend the whole flight without them." She recalled numerous other incidences of their courtship, and she had loved them all. There had been innumerable moments where intimacy was only possible because of the power of the watches. She remembered too, the nights they had spent talking long into the morning. The nights she had let her fingers stroll through her garden of pleasure, bringing herself to happy climax after climax, listening to his dulcet tones, from a phone on the other side of the country. When her hunger was fully sated, she had loved hearing his husky pants, as he took his own pleasure. Those shared moments of tenderness would never leave her, but like Patrick, she now yearned for more.

She longed to live with the man she loved, without having to dash off for another flight. She wanted to spend the night, without the thought that in hours she would be miles in the sky heading away from him with another two weeks before they would be together again.

She felt so comfortable in his arms, so loved. In her almost dreamlike state, her thoughts took her to the bargaining with the jeweler. Although her first impression of the shop had not been positive, she had warmed, to both the shop and its proprietor. The mystical feel of the shop had intrigued her. It was nothing she could actually put her finger on, but there was the feeling that almost anything was possible there.

Zachariah had a beguiling charm that had put her at her ease. She had listened to the discussion about the watches, unaware then of the full implication, though there had been an air of excitement that gripped them both, as they sat holding hands waiting patiently for the watches to be completed. The wait had been filled with the feeling that something fundamentally life changing was about to happen.

The wait was almost excruciating. Her eyes had been glued to the minute hand of the grandfather clock that stood in the corner of the shop, as it tracked slowly around the aged façade. Each minute had seemed to last an hour. After about twenty minutes, Zachariah had emerged from a small workroom at the back of the shop. He had been smiling, obviously pleased with his work.

"I think you will be pleased with the, shall we say, additional properties, of these time pieces." He had paused, seeing a slightly bemused look in his customer's eyes. "As I said earlier, I sense your problem is time. I have bound these watches in such a way it produces a *time anchor*, it is not necessary for you to know how it works only that it does work. When these watches are placed together time for the rest of the world stands still, all you have to do is be alone.

It will not work if anyone else is present. This power will give you more time together." The old man had given them a knowing smile. "Even at my age, I can see how much you want to be together. And it gives me pleasure to help." He had smiled and stroked his salt and pepper beard.

Susan had looked into his eyes and saw the sincerity. "If I may ask, why did you ask for the samples of our blood?"

She saw Zachariah's face contort in an expression of concentration. He had the look of a man who had been asked to describe *quantum physics* to some first grade students.

"It is the mix that makes the blend so potent. The mixing of blood from two people that have the simple innocent idea of *being together* has the power to move mountains...or mixed in the right way has the power to suspend time."

Susan remembered that Patrick had shifted uneasily in his seat. She knew he'd seen the potential in such a thing instantly, but the lines in his face had betrayed his concern. "The idea is marvelous, but what is the down side surely there is a danger?"

Susan loved his practical mind. He was being offered the Holy Grail and he was asking what the catch was. She hadn't been able to hide her smile. It had deepened when she saw him notice it.

Zachariah had noticed her amusement and said, "The alchemy is safe, yet there is a price. Each hour you spend in out of normal time will cost you two hours of your life," the old man stroked his beard again and added, "I do have an additional provision too, I can see how close you are and I know this is a short term solution to your problems. Rather than thinking of this as a purchase, maybe it would be better to think of this gift as a loan. I would like the opportunity to take back this power when you become engaged."

The suggestion had been met with silence. "Surely that is a small price to pay for such a gift?" Zachariah had said as he handed over the timepieces.

Susan and Patrick had smiled at each other and kissed

tenderly.

"It would seem my friends that we have a deal." Zachariah had offered his hand, which was accepted, first by Patrick and then Susan.

Susan smiled again as she remembered back to that fateful bargain.

Thoughts of the past faded into the present. She felt her lover's body pressed hard against her. She ran her hand over his chest, feeling the fine hair and the beating of his heart. She felt at home, lying naked, curled up snugly in his arms.

Patrick let out a low lusty growl. "I suppose we ought to think about rejoining the real world?" There was reluctance in his voice.

"I suppose we ought to…yet…" her voice trailed off. She stroked his chest in a soft delicate way. "Would it be so naughty, to stay here a little longer?" She used her lost little girl voice and sunk her hand to his penis. She felt him stiffen at her touch. "I think your friend here would like to stay a little longer." She gave him a friendly squeeze.

"He is not on his own. I think we should take full advantage of this extra time we have."

Susan slid on top. "Oh yes. You are right. It would be a crime to waste time. Wouldn't it?"

The Key

Jane breathed heavily. She was not a happy bunny and this was not her day. She sat at her desk, mentally growling to herself. On adjacent desks, tokens of love and affection sat proudly displayed, and David had not so much as sent an e-mail.

The other tokens had started arriving as soon as the office had opened at 8:30. Flowers, ribbon festooned boxes of chocolates, a plethora of furry toys and tokens of affection were everywhere. And even as the clock had slowly ticked round to 9:30 there was still nothing from David.

She had thought he was the one. Three years together and they seemed to get on so well. He seemed to know instinctively what she liked and more especially what she didn't like, and she didn't like this. What she would not give right now for a dozen red roses to arrive. She even thought about ordering her own, but the thought of it made her feel more miserable than she already did.

10 AM and still nothing. Her mind was not on work. Mentally she relived the good times of the past three years, walking in the park, candle light dinners, making love. God yes! There was a lot of that. They had made love in every room of his apartment and hers, including their respective linen closets. They had made love under the stars, in cars, even in an elevator. David was a very thoughtful and creative lover.

As she thought of all those happy times, she saw her desk which was bare, but for the computer, the work of the day and the small plastic tidy rack which contained her stationary odds and ends.

Her mind went over all the possibilities, all the reasons why he had not sent anything. Could he not see what an important day this was, she wondered. But how embarrassing it all was and how abandoned she felt.

10:30. Each passing sweep of the second hand seemed to take forever; she had given him the benefit of the doubt up to that point, but half way through the morning, her heart sank and a feeling of gloom hovered over her like a small black cloud. Jane thought of the things she had done for him, the card, which had cost a fortune, the gold bracelet which she had posted so it would arrive at his apartment this morning. She fumed.

11 AM. All bloody morning and still David had not bothered to contact her. She wondered if the other girls in the office noticed the sound of her fingers, as they hammered the keys, with hurt and frustration. The clock slowly clicked towards 12 noon and lunch time. Even her friend Clair had flowers on her desk. They swapped smiles across the office; she knew Clair knew all about it. This time last year it had been Jane who had comforted Clair, when her boyfriend forgot her. I guess it's my turn now, she thought.

Clair seemed to sense this too and crossed the room and walked into her cubicle, leaning against the wall. "Come on Jane, let's go out for lunch." Her voice was sympathetic and the warm hand on her shoulder was reassuring. Yet Jane was not in the mood for lunch, not in the mood for company, not in the mood for anything.

"Sorry Clair, I am not really hungry."

"Oh come on Jane, a glass of wine will make things better." Her fingers lightly stroked Jane's shoulder.

They swapped warm smiles. Jane knew her friend meant well. "It is kind of you, but I really just want to work." Jane did not want to be consoled; she really wanted to be miserable alone.

Her boyfriend of almost three years had forgotten her, on of all days, Valentines Day. The bastard.

3:30. The clock slowly ticked round in the way it does when you constantly watch it. Jane was angry but she still secretly hoped that David would come up trumps. Was it too much to hope for?

Was the lack of gift or card the message? She could not believe so. He was usually so thoughtful, he was a real gentleman, opening car doors, making all the thoughtful little gestures women found so endearing.

A cold wave washed over her, an accident? What if something had happened? Maybe it was that, that had prevented him from doing anything? She did not know whether to feel guilty or angry. She felt the other girls in the office looking at her, some smugly and others with pity. She felt sick.

4:30 arrived. She watched glumly, as one by one girls started to pack up their things as they prepared to leave for the day. Surely it was time to give up hope. Her heart sank further. How could she forgive him, even if he hadn't dumped her? She didn't know whether she was more hurt or more angry. She was reluctant to start packing up, as it signaled the loss of the last vestige of hope.

It was as she started to power down her pc, that a delivery boy called out from the office reception room, "Package for Miss Wagstaff!"

Jane stood, her heart in her mouth, waving him over. She had gone from the dark pit of despair, to the invisible choir singing the halleluiah chorus in the time it had taken for the boy to move from the door to her desk carrying that all important small parcel.

She felt like singing. She almost gave the boy a kiss.

In her mind Julie Andrews was in full "the hills are alive with the sound of music" mode. The image was shattered by the delivery boy's tentative "Miss Wagstaff? Sign here please."

Jane gave her autograph and with hands that trembled took possession of the package. The box was wrapped in brown paper, hardly the big romantic gesture, and it was light. But that was no matter the whole office could see she had not been left out. She reflected for a moment, at the size and ordinariness of the package, didn't know if that was a good sign or not. What if it was a delivery of staples? The whole office stopped to look at her, so there was no way she could open it in private. A flicker of a smile traced her lips as she remembered a happy moment when she and David had laughed together when he had threatened to send a vibrator to the office, just to see the expression on her face. Thank god it was entirely the wrong shape for that. She felt every eye in the room on her, as her nervous, yet nimble fingers tentatively opened the package. Inside the plain box a small black velvet box, with a black satin ribbon. She was so excited she felt she could wet herself. Was it a ring? On my god! Butterflies fanned their wings in her stomach as trembling fingers removed the black ribbon. She could sense the other girls straining to get a look.

Jane sprung back the lid. A gasp went around the room. As soon as she saw the contents, one thought sprung to mind and rang out clear as a bell... A key... you have to be fucking kidding? Disappointed didn't begin to describe it. It was a small bright silver key. Her key. She recognized it almost instantly, as the key to her locker at the gym. There was no mistaking it, there was a small teddy bear fob attached to the key. It had to be David sending this. Right? Who else could it be? How the fuck had he gotten the key? And why the key? No card. No message. Just the key. What was he playing at?

The girls disappeared one by one taking home their gifts and flowers. Jane could add bemused to the small growing cocktail of emotions brewing inside her. Was this all a joke that had backfired on her? She slipped on the thin jacket which completed her business suit. She casually picked up the box with the key still inside, slipping it in her pocket and made her way to her car.

As Jane set off for home she considered the gift. Maybe there was more to it than just a key? And it was a pretty box. Maybe David was trying. She couldn't quite grasp what his motive was but thought what the heck; I may as well swing past the gym, what can I lose? Curiosity doesn't always kill the cat. Right?

At her locker all looked normal. She turned the key and opened the door. There on top of her gym shoes was a rose. She smiled at the thoughtful gesture. This was much more like David. Her smile turned to a frown. Why the hell had he not sent it to the office? She took the rose from the locker and noticed a card behind. On the front it said simply, "to J." The card was definitely not from a dime store, its lavish decadence shone through the thickness of the envelope. She could see the richly embossed and gilded design of the heart on the front of the card. No doubt this had taken some thought to buy. Inside the card there was red lace and on the other side the verse.

A love that's rich, a love that's pure,

A feeling strong, that none can break,

Which lasts the twists of loves true course,

That holds you near, each moment awake,

Time for love that will endure.

Love through out, that time endures.

Beneath it was his hand written message

"Good things are always worth waiting for, Happy Valentines Day…Love… David"

Her heart leapt as she read the card. How could she not forgive the man sending her the card? She was slipping the card back in the envelope when another small box caught her eye. This time the box was in her tennis shoe. With keen anticipation and all fingers and thumbs Jane opened the box. Another key? Was this man obsessed with locks? It was a front door key, but she didn't immediately recognize it. Maybe a clue lay in the card.

She opened the card, and read the message again." Good things are always worth waiting for, Happy Valentines Day…Love… David" the message was simple and she saw no cryptic message beneath the text.

A wave of happiness swept over her. At least it was David, she thought, as she looked at the rose. At least he had not forgotten. The day in the office seemed less important now. She held the rose in her hand, felt the hard stem, and held the soft blossom with its velvety petals up to her nose and smelt its exquisite perfume. It somehow compensated and she felt herself relax. The bitter anger that had been there melted. There was still a pang of disappointment, all the girls in the office still thought she was "Jenny-no-boyfriend" and David still had some distance to travel before he would put that right.

Slowly Jane turned the key in her palm and as she looked at it the fluorescent lights of the gym reflected on its shiny surface. Surely it wasn't to his apartment. But what else could it be to?

This had to be a game, some form if scavenger hunt. A determined smile crossed her lips. Well she was going to have to go over to his place anyway. Her smile led to the ironic thought, that it would be rude not to thank him for the card and flowers. Maybe then she would discover why he wanted to play this cloak and dagger game.

It occurred to her, how easily he was manipulating her. She should be furious, shouldn't she? Yet the ice was melting, just a little.

It was a short drive from the gym to his apartment on the swanky side of town. As she locked the car door and walked up the drive to the block of apartments, she felt a little self conscious. She should have gone home to shower and change, she was still in her work clothes and she felt a little grubby.

His car was there, so he was at home. Jane smoothed the

creases from her skirt, with her hand, and then fiddled with her hair as she approached the door. She hesitated for a fleeting moment, to stand or run?

Running was never an option. Three years together, she was just being silly, and a little nervous. Surely a man as resourceful as David would have something wonderful in mind.

Jane held her breath, as she pressed the door bell. She waited. No reply. She waited some more, and pressed the bell again. Still no reply. Had he gone to the shops? She looked back down the drive at his car. The nearest shops were quite a walk. She waited again.

The wait had been about ten minutes. She fiddled with the keys in her jacket pocket realizing there in her hand was both the question and solution. Jane fumbled with the key she'd retrieved from her gym locker. Slowly she slipped it into the lock and turned it. The door opened.

As she stepped across the threshold, she played the scenarios through her head. Was it a game? Was he ill? He could be lying unconscious in the apartment, which would explain the reason for him not phoning. Wouldn't it?

"David?" Her ears were acutely tuned for any sound.

Nothing, "David, are you here?"

Still nothing.

She had been in the apartment many times and had always felt comfortable. This felt different, a bit like looking through her parents bedroom; not exactly wrong, but not exactly right. It was a feeling she felt uneasy with. Curiously she opened the door to the dining room. The now setting sun cast a reddish tint over the room. Casting her eyes round she noticed the table set for an elaborate dinner, a candlelight dinner for two.

At the spot where she usually sat when the dined at his apartment, just below the pressed white linen napkin there was another key. Another bloody key? What was it, with all the keys? She picked it up and looked carefully at the precious object. It was a small gold key on a delicate golden chain. It was fine work.

There was a click and the front door opened and closed. She hurriedly put the gold key and chain back where she had found it fussing that it was not in the right place. Her heart stopped. For one nasty moment she thought 'what if all this isn't for me? What if it is all one ghastly mistake?'

She turned and there stood David in the doorway, wine in hand and the broadest grin she had ever seen him wear.

"We needed something special to help celebrate" he said by way of an explanation, brandishing the bottle of imported French Champagne.

"What exactly are we celebrating?" Jane asked, with just a little frost in her voice. She looked him up and down appraising his choice of clothes. He looked delightfully casual in jeans and open neck shirt beneath a soft green cashmere sweater. She was also delighted that he was wearing the bracelet she had sent as his Valentines Day gift. She mentally drew the comparison between his clothes and her rather stuffy office-wear.

David smiled, and put the bottle down on a small table, before walking over to her. He tenderly held her shoulders, feeling the warm skin beneath her thin blouse as he kissed her. "There are many things to celebrate. Not least of which is that it is Valentines Day and we are together. I have prepared a meal for us and it is a lovely night." He looked into her eyes and kissed her softly again.

Jane smiled. He had a point, yet the day couldn't be forgotten quite so easily. Why couldn't he have called earlier? Why had he put her through all that today? He'd deliberately made her think he'd forgotten. Men could really be bloody irritating. There was something charming in the way he disarmed her though.

She loved the way he took control and ushered her to a comfy chair. She accepted the seat along with the offered chilled glass of Pinot Grigio

He sank to his knees before her and eased off her shoes "Dinner is prepared. All is in hand. There is plenty of time for you to relax before we eat." Still cradling her foot in his large hand, he began to massage the ball of her foot. He felt her tension. Her skin felt tight and hard, as his fingers worked into her skin through her nylons. He sensed she felt a little uncomfortable coming straight from work and him handling her feet. He lifted her foot up and lowered his head down and kissed her instep, showing her it was ok, and this simple act seemed to reassure her. She visibly sank back into the chair and yielded to his masterful touch

"It's ok. Just let the hassles of the day drift away." He felt her relax, as his large firm hands manipulated her feet, fingers softly pushing her nylons between her toes, separating them each in turn. He looked up watching as with a sigh of contentment her eyes drifted closed and she surrendered herself completely to him. He felt proud to have this woman feel this comfortable with him. He found this power, freely given to him very exhilarating and very erotic, and his penis responded to his heartfelt emotions.

She felt at ease, relaxed and comfortable with giving this man total control. She felt his fingers part her toes, and felt his hands covering her feet which were small in comparison. She closed her eyes and enjoyed the moment, splaying her toes, like a contented cat. To give this much control to someone excited her and that familiar tingle began to build slowly from deep within.

She must have dozed but was brought back to the here and now, by the soft tones of David's voice. "Time for dinner." She looked up into his eyes, and smiled.

David smiled back and offered his hand, helping her from the leather armchair and escorting her to the dining table. There was light classical music playing in the background and the candles on the table had been lit as she'd dozed. She noticed the small key that had been at her place setting earlier was no longer there. She was going to say something but the starters arrived. Shrimp on a nest of soft salad greens, with a light dressing. She waited for David to take his place. With a smile and a light nod of his head, as if being given permission she started. The prawns were delightful, soft and delicate, the greens, complementing them with a slightly spicy peppery taste which was highly pleasant to her pallet.

David loved shrimp. They were always a safe first course.

He loved to watch Jane eat; she seemed to savor every bite. He loved the expression on her face when she liked a taste. It was the look of a child tasting something for the very first time, even though she must have eaten shrimp a thousand times before.

The first course consumed David leaned closer, smiled and asked, "How was your day? Good day at work?"

"Well," Jane paused, smiled, and had a sip of wine. By the tone in his voice she could tell he was teasing her in a nice way and baiting her like this was part of his sense of humor so she decided to take the question in the spirit it was intended. "It started a little shakily. The morning was a little disappointing…." She paused again searching for just the right tone. "Things have been getting steadily better." She paused again waiting for David to say something. As it was obvious he was not going to fill the void, she continued, "And what about you? Have you had a good day?"

With a smile he replied "Yes I had a lovely morning. I took the day off work to do a little shopping, to prepare for a meal. I spent a little time at the gym. Yes all in all so far the day has been fine." David could not hide his amusement. He loved that they were so in tune. He had worried that she might not have seen the funny side of the morning's game, fake abandonment. He was sure she had been very irritated at the time.

He never wanted her to feel hurt, but he knew to mildly aggravate someone could have its advantages, not the least of which could be found in bed.

The second course was chicken in a light creamy mushroom sauce with mashed potatoes and garden peas with thin strips of buttered carrots. He had thought a light meal, and was delighted that his partner seemed to be enjoying it as much as he was. The combination of the soft creamed potatoes and crispy vegetables made the textures of the meal interesting. The tastes were rich and a delight to their taste buds.

David watched as she parted her lips to receive a morsel of chicken. A dribble of sauce hit her chin. His mind jumped ahead an hour or so drawing parallels. He felt himself stiffen at the thought.

Jane looked up into his eyes, dabbing the sauce from her chin. She knew what he was thinking. She could feel him undressing her, with those big brown eyes of his and was glad she had worn her favorite lace bra and panty set; her come and fuck me now set.

She was sure he had been looking at the lacy shapes through her white blouse since he had walked into the room. The way he looked at her made her tingle and moisten between the legs. She returned the look.

Was it her imagination? His tongue seemed to dance on the mashed potato on his fork. Or was it wishful thinking. She imagined him using that tongue on her in the way he always did. She pressed her thighs together and as she did she was very aware of the effect, she could feel the moisture soaking her panties. He was oh so very oral.

He looked up from his last mouthful of food. Although their plates were empty, he could see she was as hungry as he was. He could see her nipples outlined clearly against the thin fabric of her blouse. He smiled to himself. Dessert would have to wait. With the thought of dessert a seed was planted in his mind. Yes dessert. Mmmmm. Yes that would be fun.

"There is another course but I think it can wait for a little later?" He asked it as a question but the tone in his voice made it more of a suggestion.

"That was a lovely meal, thank you." Jane dabbed her lips with the napkin, folded it and laid it beside her plate, in contrast to the way he crumpled his and tossed it down. They rose from the table together and stepped jointly into a soft, yet passionate kiss. For her there was a feeling of them having waited quite long enough. All the feelings of irritation had vanished with the meal. She loved this man, with all his quirky ways.

He felt her warmth pressed against his body. As they kissed his hands stroked her back, unconsciously mapping the terrain, from the wisps of hair at her collar, down her shoulders and across the soft cotton fabric of her blouse to the indents of her bra strap to the little bulge where the hooks and eyes came together. His hands caressed the warm hollow of her back enjoying the feel of her warm skin through her blouse. His hand slid past the top of her skirt noticing the different texture of the material as his hand moved onto her ass, and what a beautiful ass it was.

She loved the way he held her. She felt so secure in his arms, felt as though she was protected from the world. She loved her body being explored by David's big firm hands. She loved the feeling of being possessed, totally consumed by his power and his desire. Her fingers felt his muscular back, the strength, the raw masculinity. Everything about him, made her want him. His scent was a potent manliness mixed with subtle aftershave.

His kiss deepened and her mouth opened to accept the invader. Tongues danced their soft, slow, erotic ballet. Her hands pulled him closer to her receptive body, one hand on his ribs and the other on his tight muscular ass. She felt his big erection pushing into her and she wanted him. Now!

He felt her urgency and swept her up in his arms and carried her through an adjacent door to the bedroom. She made no protest as he laid her on the bed. There would be time for slow lovemaking later, they could wait no longer. They wanted each other too much for foreplay and niceties.

Still dressed and with her panties pulled aside he lay atop her. He wanted her so badly. He felt her soft form beneath him as he eased himself into position. He penetrated her easily. She was wet, open and yet so pleasingly tight. His strokes were languid to start with. He wanted her, but wanted it to last. The paradox of passion, like a meal to be savored, still a voracious appetite makes even connoisseurs devour a meal all too quickly.

He built rapidly to his full stroke. He loved the sensation of his whole member sliding in and out. His hips rolled as he did, wanting Jane to climax with him. A bead of sweat dripped from his brow. He grunted with exertion and concentration wanting things to last, but surely that climax could not be that far away. He felt his balls tighten.

She felt his power. The surge as he took her. She loved the feeling of being taken, the feeling of him above her. She bit her lip and raked her nails against his back. She gave herself most willingly, a sacrificial lamb on the altar of Eros. His weight pushed her into the bed. She responded to him pushing back grinding her pubis into his. She felt exultant in this act of passion.

She caught her breath with every ardent thrust. Her own climax seemed to build from his first possession of her, building in waves with each powerful thrust. She was close and she knew that he was too. She could hear his grunts and moans of passion in her ear. Her hips rose to meet his. She wanted to fuck him as hard as he was fucking her.

The tingling that had started earlier over dinner had been steadily growing. It grew from within and rippled along her spine and touched all of her, from her flushed cheek to the very tip of her toes. The sugar and vinegar waves lapped against the shore, growing with their lustful thrusts. Wave after wave built until there was nothing but the swirling mass of foam, the tingling that washed through and over her in a shower of stars.

David's own climax pulsed through him, an exultant

thrust and groan, as his very essence drained from him. The sweet and sour pulse swept over him and he stayed perfectly still, panting, Jane impaled fully upon him.

Slowly coming down from the ecstasy of climax, David felt spent, though he was still erect and still fully inside his love. He was aware of her vagina gently milking his penis. He was now also aware of his weight on her. Supporting his own weight he rolled onto his side taking Jane with him, not wanting to break their connection. One hand stroking her hair, he kissed her deeply. It felt so right when her lips parted and she returned the kiss.

Their bodies entwined, Jane stroked his muscular thigh, feeling his hard toned body though his clothes. Her hand slowly mapped the contours of his body, his firm tight ass. She could not resist a squeeze. Her breath came in rasps, as she noticed did David's. Her skin glowed with perspiration making her blouse stick to her body. It was funny how it could feel kind of gross and fantastic all at the same time. She felt warm and comfortable and so relaxed, not wanting to move. It was obvious from his contented smile that David felt the same, so they stayed entwined on the bed.

"I love you" he said smiling that warm post coital smile.

Jane felt the warm flush of climax on her cheek as she returned his smile "I love you too, you are very special to me you know."

He smiled and looked into her eyes. There was no need to answer. It was very obvious how they both felt. He held her close to his body, aware of their breathing which had grown deeper with the exertion of their lovemaking. "I could stay here forever."

"Yes that would be nice." Jane rolled in and kissed his cheek.

David ran his fingers through her hair "I am going to make love to you all night."

"Mmmmmmmmmm," Jane purred. "I like the sound of that. I guess we should take our clothes off?"

"All in good time," David said, still smiling and stroking her hair. "I want this to last, all of this to last." He leaned in and kissed her lips. "I am going to make love to you. But first I have had an idea for dessert."

Jane let out a little chuckle. The idea was kind of silly to combine making love and dessert. But what the heck, she thought. "Ok, what is for dessert?"

Rather theatrically he announced like the maître d' in a top restaurant, "For the last course of our meal may I present imported strawberries and whipped cream."

"Sounds yummy," Jane purred.

"Even more so with the way I plan to serve them."

"Oh yes?"

David flashed her his wicked, this is a new one smile. "Yes, I am going to dip them in our love cream and we will eat them warm together."

Jane could not hold back another girlish giggle. God he was creative, and she loved his playful nature. "Sounds yummy. I can't wait." She kissed his lips. "Thank you David for such a lovely evening... I love you"

"I love you too. I want us always to be together."

They held each other tight.

"I have something for you." David fumbled under the pillow and produced another small box. "For you," he said. With the push of a small button the box flipped open.

As the box opened she caught her breath, inside was a ring and the small key on the chain. It was beautiful. The ring was every girl's dream. The center was comprised of three dark green emeralds and around them were sparkling diamonds. She didn't count them but there were a lot. They all sparkled in the rich gold setting, as light caught the facets as she turned the ring in her fingers. The colors lit up her face. It was all too much. She felt a tear in her eye.

His voice cut through her thoughts. "Will you marry me?"

A flood of emotions overcame Jane and she burst into tears. She held him close and whispered a simple "yes" into his ear. "I love you," she whispered as her mouth found his and they shared a deep and passionate kiss.

"Here, let me help." David took the ring and offered it to her finger, sliding it smoothly over her knuckle. It was a perfect fit.

Jane stared at the ring transfixed. It was so beautiful. As she looked at the shiny cluster of diamonds and emeralds, emotions overwhelmed her. How could the day that had started so badly have ended like this, a dream come true?

Something caught her mind in the way things do.

"I have a question, how did you get my locker key?"

David propped himself up a little on one elbow, "I have to say, that was a bit tricky. I had to enlist the help of your friend Clair."

"She was in on this?" Her voice was a little louder than she had intended.

Her affronted tone worried him and he smiled reassuringly and ran his fingers through her hair "no, not in on it. All Clair knew was I intended a surprise in your locker, she knew nothing more, she knew nothing about this—" he dipped his gaze from her eyes to the ring, and back again. "She knew nothing. Only that I wanted to surprise you."

Jane smiled, reassured by his words. "There is one thing I don't understand," Jane said smiling quizzically. "The keys? What was it with all the keys?"

David smiled and kissed her, "Oh quite simple really. The key to my heart. Happy Valentines day…"

They kissed for a long time before David whispered, "Time for strawberries!"

Afterward

The community that includes people with an interest in domination and submission is a much misunderstood and unusual world to the uninitiated.

A friend of mine described D/s in a story in terms of "an old-fashioned marriage." A deeply committed Christian couple I know told me that they saw no conflict between high Christian values and a D/s lifestyle.

The insider of this lifestyle is usually either amused or irritated by the perceptions of the outsider. I consider myself very non-judgemental and believe that people should pursue happiness in whatever form it comes, without fear of condemnation from others.

In my opinion, relationships that have their foundation in dominance and submission, are just like most other relationships. They all seem to suffer from the same problems and hassles about work, money and everything else our society throws at us. At their very best, D/s relationships are beautiful relationships filled with respect, trust and love.

It has been my privilege to know a number of people in this lifestyle and they have never given me the impression that they were anything other than normal people who have different tastes. It has been a constant irritant to me that the world of D/s, portrayed by the news and media, is a world of weird people, who are hell bent on inflicting nonconsensual pain and committing, brutal, sadistic acts on each other. I just do not believe the facts bear this out.

Once you know what to look for in people's behavior, you might be surprised how many of the people you meet have D/s tendencies, even if they do not live this lifestyle. I would bet there is at least one couple you know that has experimented in this world. I am willing to bet that armed with this knowledge you will never view your neighbour in the same light again.

I would ask you the reader, to read the story without prejudice. I hope you will see in this story just a different way of life. I have tried to write this novel showing the key factors that in my opinion make a relationship, D/s or otherwise, work. Love, trust, respect and commitment are the crucial elements in both vanilla and D/s relationships.

The Anniversary

An Excerpt from The Crimson Z

Chapter One

The brilliant white headlights from Evelyn's Jaguar cut through the darkness as she drove through the night. Her only companion on this cold night was a single red rose, which sat on the passenger seat. Her knuckles were tight, as her nervous fingers gripped the leather-covered steering wheel.

Her sumptuous, silk stockinged, thighs rubbed together pleasingly as she changed gears. Wearing silk stockings had always aroused her. The tightness of the darker band at the top of her thigh and the way it hugged her securely made her legs feel lovingly restrained, making her whole body pulse and tingle with excitement.

It had been twelve months to the day since she had last met with her clandestine lover. The tension that was coiled within her was beginning to show as she neared her destination. She checked her clothing for the thousandth time, since getting dressed that afternoon.

Peter's instructions had been precise, what to wear, and when to change into it. This had done nothing to help her nervousness and anticipation of their meeting.

Peter was a stickler for detail, and she found it easy to comply with his dress code. Her crisp white, linen blouse and smart black A-line skirt did not look out of place from her normal office attire. For many years now, she had worn stockings and garter belt, so that was not unusual either.

Late in the afternoon, she had changed into the final items. These she only wore on this day of the year now. Their touch on her skin felt unusual now, yet strangely comforting.

She squirmed against the Jaguar's leather seat, as the chain caressed her intimately. She looked at the amber lighted digital clock. She looked at the mileage counter willing it to speed up. Time passed incredibly slowly making her feel like a small child on her way to the seaside; constantly asking are we there yet?

Her mind drifted back over the challenging day she had spent at the office and the assortment of problems she had tackled. She contemplated the duality of her nature, her assertiveness in the office and the passivity when she was with Peter. She drew similar parallels between Peter and James, the two men she loved, but who were so different.

This early evening meeting had been her main focus for the past week and she had hardly been able to think of anything else. As the amber digits ticked relentlessly by, and she neared her destination the tension she felt rose to a crescendo.

As she drove, Evelyn went through her mental checklist. Had she dressed correctly? Was she fully prepared? God she hoped so. Peter had always been a stickler for detail and would notice a hair out of place. Yet again, as she went through her cerebral preparations, she felt a moistness, a liquid glow, like her very core was melting and with these feelings of desire, came a gut wrenching pang of guilt.

Suddenly a cold rush, swept over her. How could she betray her husband? How could she be unfaithful to such a good man, for this one night of passion? With a lump in her throat, she thought of James, and their three-year marriage and the vows she was breaking. Yet tonight, as she had done for the past four years, she would give herself totally to Peter and nothing on earth could or would stop her from making that rendezvous.

She loved James dearly. Their three-year marriage was a

happy one. James was a good man, a loving and caring partner. He was a very straightforward man, uncomplicated. He was the type that if he said something, you knew he meant it. If he promised to do something, he would do it. She loved James for all that he was, yet there was one thing he was not, and could never be. He was not her Master. She had only ever had one Master. Peter.

Her love for Peter was not the same as her love for James. She loved James with her heart but Peter she loved with her very soul.

The one thing that had united her two lovers was their love for her, but the two men in her life were entirety different in nature and temperament. There was a hard edge to Peter, something uncompromising. He had a natural authority about him. He was and always had been every inch the man in control.

The flash of a rabbit darting across the road brought her back to the here and now. The rumble of the tires on asphalt lulled her back to her thoughts.

Evelyn had been married to Peter when she had met James. She had known James for years before she had married him and until then had always thought of him as a good friend. Their three-year marriage had only deepened her feelings for James.

James was altogether softer and a much more tender person, a man that loved her unconditionally just as she was. In return, she loved him. She knew he loved every inch of her soft rounded body, by the attention he lavished upon her. Yet, he was not a demanding man. He always put her needs first, which was very nice, though slightly irritating at times, as she much preferred assertive men.

Her mother had described him once as "Low maintenance" He was a man that despite her flaws would always be there for her. Making love to James, was soft and tender, he never neglected any morsel of her. His tastes though were pure vanilla, missionary with the occasional oral gratification, which he was happy to reciprocate.

They first met at work. James worked in the same office block as she did, though not for the same firm, and their lunch hours had coincided. She soon came to think of him, as the big brother she had never had. Their shared lunches had been a pleasant thing to look forward to each day. They laughed freely over a coffee and sandwiches for years. That had been a happy time, which she always looked back on with fondness.

Then there was a time when they no longer met for lunch. Dark Clouds had descended in her life. It had been a bleak and stormy time, and Evelyn had retreated to a place deep within herself. It had been a time when there was no light in the day, a time when she had wanted to die. A time when she had been a soulless shell. It was in this that depth of despair that James had found her. He had breathed life into her again, bringing her back from the edge. He had brought her back into the light, helping her to see the joy of the new day and helping her to laugh again. That was four years ago now.

The engine growled and Evelyn changed to a lower gear, as the road became more winding. She knew she was close to her destination now and she felt the pang of hunger in her stomach and the all too familiar ache between her thighs. She could not wait to be with Peter.

Peter, had been and still was, her passion. Evelyn had known him for what had seemed like forever. She had known him for years before she had ever met James. Theirs had been a whirlwind romance, flowers, candle light dinners, moon light trysts. As their relationship deepened Peter's nature and his strength came to the fore. Evelyn swallowed, as she heard the words in her head *"Love, honor, and obey."*

Evelyn had been brought up to believe in sexual equality, and she did believe, but there had been something missing in her life when she met Peter. From the very start, there was a power with Peter, not a menacing power to be sure, but an authority. This was not a simple macho manifestation, but a deep-rooted natural power, a light that drew Evelyn like a moth to a flame.

It had started easily enough at an electronics trade show, she was there as the personal assistant for a corporate buyer. The meetings that she had attended had finished and she was free to browse around the exhibition. She looked around curiously although in truth electronic gadgets left her a bit cold. Across the room, she saw Peter. Their eyes met and there was an instant connection. There was a delicious flirtation as they played from across the room. Eventually Evelyn made her way to the stand where Peter was giving a demonstration of a highly complicated piece of equipment. The customer moved on, Peter stepped up to Evelyn and introduced himself. His smile that day would be burned into her memory for all eternity.

Evelyn's partners before Peter had been few. In those days of stick thin models, not everyone appreciated her fuller figure. Those who had, had left her feeling unfulfilled and that sex was overrated. The early dates and dinners with Peter were much like those she'd had in the past, with the exception that Peter had not pounced on her at the end of the first date. A simple tender kiss had sufficed at the end of the date. In fact, after the third date she had begun to worry that Peter was not as attracted to her as she was to him and it had been Evelyn that made the first move.

After dinner, she had invited him back for coffee. He browsed her CD collection as she rattled coffee cups in the kitchen. She asked him how he liked his coffee; he replied strong, black and no sugar.

Evelyn returned with a tray, with cups and a café tire. They sipped coffee for a while. Peter looked totally at ease as he sat on the couch. Evelyn, by contrast was nervous and fidgeting. What was he waiting for? Surely he could see she wanted him, yet there he sat, pleasantly smiling and making small talk. She flirted with him, trying to add suggestive snippets like, "I have always been into bedroom design, it allows you to express yourself," into the conversation. She had expected a response like "I would be interested to see how you have decorated yours." However, no such response had been forthcoming.

It was obvious to her that Peter was interested, yet he took none of the opportunities to follow up with a suggestive comment of his own. The attraction was obvious yet he did not make a move.

They finished the coffee and she felt it was now or never. She wanted Peter and she knew that Peter wanted her. With a tremble in her voice, she said, "I would like you to stay."

"I would like that very much," he answered, his tone warm, yet authoritative. His tone made her tingle.

"Shall I slip into something more comfortable?" There was a noticeable quaver in her voice.

"I think you are fine as you are." There was something in Peter's voice that put him firmly in control. "I would like you to stand." The politeness in his request did not hide the fact that it was an instruction.

She smiled and stood, a little shakily. She had always been a little self-conscious about her body. Her teenage years had done nothing for her self-esteem. Back then, she had dreaded going to the swimming pool, even though she loved the water and loved to swim. In a swimsuit, she had felt so exposed, vulnerable, and very aware that her body was not the type found in the glossy teen magazines. As a teenager thoughts of communal showers with the other girls, had made her feel physically sick. Many nights she had cried herself to sleep, dreaming of the sylph like body she would never have. The cruel jibes made her frustrated and angry.

This was before therapy. During the many hours of therapy, she had come to realize her size 18 dress size was not at all abnormal and her Monroe like curves were not bad although they simply did not comply to the stereotypical pencil thin models in Vogue.

Yet even with her new layer of confidence, there was a

tingle of apprehension that climbed up her spine, as the fear of being judged reasserted itself.

She looked at Peter, who was passively, yet happily, looking at her. Her confidence grew again, as she contemplated her own figure. She was well proportioned, her figure resembling an hourglass. She had always been proud of her trim well-turned ankles and shapely calves.

She loved the curve of her hips and the swell of her bottom that had attracted more than one wolf whistle from construction sites. It was her ample breasts that seemed to attract most men though. She had no need of silicone, her breasts were totally natural and they were still firm at 30. Sure, there were things she would change if she had a magic wand. She would wish away an inch or so from her upper thighs, maybe tighten and tone in the odd area, but there would be no going under the surgeon's knife for her.

As Evelyn stood before Peter, she assessed her own looks, more critically than any partner would. She looked at Peter, trying to read his mind. What was he thinking? She felt more than a little self-conscious. It was like stripping away the therapy sessions and going back to her days at school. She felt the weight of her nerves once more. Confidence ebbed and flowed, like breakers on the shore.

She looked to Peter for reassurance. As she looked more deeply into Peter's eyes, she bathed in the warmth of his smile. She could plainly see now, that far from judging her, he looked more like he was about to eat her up. She wondered if he knew that she could see a flick of tongue as he licked his lips. He looked as if he planned to devourer her, and she hoped to God that he was going to do it soon.

She became less self aware as she turned her attentions to him. She felt drawn to his handsomely rugged features. He looked impressively strong and she wondered how his body would feel pressed hard against her.

Evelyn was hungry and she wanted Peter. The wait was making her feel impatient. The anticipation was torture, the tension building, making her want to scream, if only inside.

Her eyes had been fixed on his intense gaze, and suddenly her attention switched back to herself. She was standing there like a schoolgirl. She found herself fidgeting, smoothing her skirt to remove the creases that didn't exist; she looked at herself fiddling with the buttons on her cuffs, then played with her hair nervously and smiled at him. Yet now, in a strange way, she was beginning to enjoy this feeling of unease. In fact, she found this to be a big part of this brand new experience.

Her reflection was interrupted by Peter, "I like things a certain way, I hope you don't mind." Peter was calm and sat still, totally relaxed with the situation, a smile playing across his lips, "I have a feeling that you and I are very compatible."

"I hope so." Evelyn felt the blood rush to her cheeks as her heart pumped madly. She looked into the eyes of this tall handsome man, trying to see into his mind. She was nervous, yet more excited by this, than she had ever been with any man before. She felt her nipples dilate and was sure Peter could see just how excited she was. Her eyes flickered for a moment to his trousers; there was no mistaking the bulge. She was pleased to have this effect on him.

His eyes fixed on hers, "I hope so too." Peter's lips curled into a natural smile. There was a flash of white teeth and the soft edge of affection in his voice. He leaned back in the chair and crossed his legs. "I would like you to do something for me, but it must be done freely." His eyes never broke contact with hers as he spoke.

She shifted her weight slightly from one foot to the other and said, "What would you like me to do?" The tremble in her voice was half in fear of the answer and half in anticipation. Right here and now she would do anything. Her eyes were locked to his. She was drawn like a moth to the flame.

Peter uncrossed his legs and leaned forward, "Firstly, I would like you to take off your blouse."

Evelyn was not used to men being this direct with her, she felt a second rush of blood to her cheeks, but it excited her beyond belief and she felt herself moisten. Was it wrong of her to do as he asked, she wondered. Yet, it felt so right, how could she not comply?

Her heart beat faster as her nervous fingers fumbled with difficult buttons. Her mind flicked to a time in school changing rooms and other girls laughing at her developing body. She had been the first in her class to develop breasts and had been teased endlessly for it. As she loosened the blouse from her skirt, she relived every negative comment she had ever heard. Was Peter going to judge her? How much easier sex would be with the lights off.

She shook as the garment slipped from her shoulders and fell to the floor. She was revealed. Her mind raced. Where was this going? She knew it would end in sex, but this was so different from the usual courtship ritual. Would the sex be that much different too?

In contrast to Evelyn, Peter looked and sounded contented and relaxed. "And now your skirt please." His voice was calm and measured, his face placid. Evelyn found her gaze slipping from his eyes to the prominent bulge in his trousers. She felt flustered, and she contemplated sinking to her knees there and then and releasing the captive. However, the instruction had not been given and she was not brave enough to deviate from Peter's word.

She wondered what her friends would say, if she told them, a man had told her to do this and she had complied. Indeed, could she ever tell anyone how much it excited her to give this control to a man? Nice girls didn't do such things. Did they?

She had undressed in front of men before, but usually the man would be busy removing his clothes at the same time. This felt more personal. She was under the spotlight; it was her performing for him. Trembling fingers grappled with the belligerent fastening of the skirt, she quietly muttered under her breath as the clasp surrendered and the skirt puddled at her feet. Evelyn looked closely at Peter looking for any reaction negative or otherwise, as her thighs were now revealed. To her relief, Peter's gaze traced admiringly up her legs and the swell in his trousers confirmed, in a most honest way, he liked what he saw. Again, her nerves twitched and she wished this first time had been beneath the cover of a darkened room.

She looked at Peter and his eyes were still fixed on her. It was obvious that he was amused by the struggle with the skirt's clasp, yet he only kept a slight smile, not wanting to break the sensuality of the moment. "Your shoes please."

Evelyn looked down at her shoes. A part of her wanted to resist. This was wrong, wasn't it? It was wrong for a man to issue instructions for her to strip, wasn't it? She was not a whore, to do as she was told, a plaything, a life-size, queen-sized, Barbie doll. Yet this was compulsive. Peter was no monster, quite the opposite. He had a charming way about him. He was a gentleman. She felt like she was being charmed out of her clothes, but there was something compelling in the way he talked. Something in the matter-of-fact way, he asked her to remove each garment that made it impossible to refuse. She felt his glance alter from warm to steely, the longer she delayed, though in truth from request to action it was a fraction of a second. Peter was almost motionless, yet the glint in his eye and the power of his voice made each request overwhelming.

She was confused why the removal of the shoes was so symbolic, was it the reduction of height? Or her feeling of helplessness? Evelyn took a deep breath and steadied her nerve. She slipped into the abyss, as the shoes were gently slid off and she stood before him in bra, panties and pantyhose. Now resigned to her fate, she felt the sooner she was naked the better, then at least there would be the love making. Evelyn went to remove her bra, but Peter stopped her.

"Not until I am ready, please. You may remove it, but only when I ask you," he continued with cool measured voice.

Evelyn was confused, he didn't want to see her naked? "I don't understand, Peter."

Peter leaned forward, "This will happen all in good time, but it will happen in my time. I would like you to do as I ask." There was no anger in his voice, just the opposite; it was a calm response, which Evelyn found comforting rather than upsetting. "I want to savor you, as I would a gourmet meal. Which is better filet mignon or hamburger?" Peter clasped his hands together and studiously steepled his fingers "Which would you like me to consider you? Filet or burger?"

Evelyn needed no time to think "Filet." She had been regarded as a burger, too many times in the past.

Peter leaned back in the seat again. "Are you ready to continue?"

"Yes Peter." She looked directly at her lover.

Peter returned her smile and said, "I have a request. I have certain tastes and it would please me, very much, if you would address me as Sir. It is a simple word that shows respect. It is a word that shows me you are ready and willing to serve. The choice to serve is for you to make, and this is a choice you must make freely. It will feel a bit strange at first, but it is a way some people live their lives. It is a way I live mine.

"I have a profound feeling that you would take to this lifestyle. I feel deep down, that you have a need to serve. I know you have a need to please me. Do you feel you are you ready to take this first step? Do you feel you are ready to do as I ask? To please me?"

Though she was unsure in her mind of the implications of what it meant to serve, without hesitation she replied, "Yes Sir." The sir came out of her lips naturally, as an involuntary reaction to his authority and she liked the way it sounded, respectful and comforting. She was aware again of the moistness in her panties and she knew there would be no hiding it from Peter.

"Good girl," Peter said, with a flash of white teeth. Then his lips set to a warm smile.

"May I ask a question?"

"Of course, you may ask anything."

"What does it mean to serve? What is it I have to do?"

Without hesitation Peter replied, "To serve me well, requires you to do as I ask, when I ask you to do it. This requires you to trust me. I wish you to follow my requests carefully, without question, because you know it is what I wish. In serving me, it also fulfills a side of you that has not yet been fulfilled. This is very much a two way street. You must want to serve. You must want to trust. In return, our love for each other will blossom."

Reassured by his words, but still a little apprehensive she asked, "What if I fail? What if I can't live up to all you expect?"

Peter took her hand and kissed it his warm lips grazed her flesh, "I want this as much for you, as I do for myself. It is not an audition to be passed. You need to want to do this. You need to feel in your heart that this is right for you. In return, I will support you, nurture you, guide you, and hold you.

"I feel that you have been repressing these feelings of submission, a little like a caged bird. I want you to be the person that I know you have locked away deep inside you. I want you to be that person for you.

"It will seem a little strange at first, giving me that power over you. In time, and with trust, it will become second nature for you. With trust, you will focus on your service to me. I in turn will devote my life to cherishing you. Trust is needed because you have to know instinctively that what I ask you to do will not harm you. You will find a deep sense of well being in your service. But it is your service to give freely."

Peter paused for a moment, to let the depth of his words sink in. With a kind warm tone in his voice he continued, "I ask you again, freely and happily would you choose to serve me?"

Evelyn searched her mind. Yes, she wanted him. Yes, she was burning with desire, but more than that, much more, she knew within her very soul that the only truth that mattered was, she loved Peter more profoundly than she had ever loved before. "Yes Sir I am willing to serve. I will do all you ask of me and I will try to serve you as well as I can."

"I can ask nothing more from you than that. This makes me very happy Evelyn, very happy indeed."

"Sir, what would you ask of me?"

Peter paused for a moment, "I am not fond of pantyhose, I would be happier if you never wore them again. Stockings are fine, but I just don't like pantyhose. I would be disappointed to find you wearing them." His words were friendly, yet Evelyn was in no doubt that his likes and dislikes must be taken seriously. There was an undeniable throbbing at her center. Her clit ached to be touched.

The suspense from what was happening was incredible. Never before in her life had she been so turned on, so very aware of her body and her needs. Right there and then she would give anything to have Peter rip off her remaining clothes and fuck her. Yet she knew she would have to wait for his instruction.

"I wish you to remove your pantyhose, please." Peter spoke as if he was at the dinner table asking her to pass the salt, yet as much as it sounded a request; there was no getting away from the power of his tone.

Evelyn looked down, as she hooked her thumbs under the elastic of the hose. She tried to make the removal as elegant as she could for Peter. Boyfriends in the past had never paused at this stage; they were so intent to getting at what was inside. There was such an awkwardness about getting them off that she vowed never to wear them again. Having removed the garment she stood head lowered, looking at her body.

She wished at that moment that she was a size 10, but the fact remained that she wasn't and with Peter looking at her with the *I am going to eat you for breakfast* look in his eye she realized, maybe for the first time in her life, she really didn't give a shit. This man lusted after her as she was, and she wanted him inside her. Size was irrelevant. She was hungry.

She was so excited she was about to explode. Her nipples were painfully hard where they pressed against the flimsy fabric of her bra. Peter would be able to see how hard they were. A glance down showed her panties were every bit as embarrassingly wet as she feared they would be. Peter would be able to see that too. Calmly she waited for his next instruction.

"Please look up," again in his tone was friendly.

She happily obeyed and their eyes met again. She looked closely at him, his face showed its 35 years. Though clean shaven, at this stage in the evening a light shadow was on his chin. His hair, a chestnut brown was neatly trimmed but slightly mussed from where he had run his fingers through it during the course of the evening. Evelyn saw warmth and kindness on his face. She returned his gaze and licked her lips in anticipation. This wait was a tantalizing game of tease and denial that was delicious.

Without her power suit, she felt more vulnerable, but the way Peter looked at her made her feel strong again and she minded less that he could see her like this. She switched her gaze from herself to Peter's face and then to his groin. He made no effort to try to hide his erection, which strained against the fabric of his trousers. Here was a man at home with his body.

She felt Peter's savoring of her body... She felt his eyes linger on her ample breasts and the fact that he could see her erect nipples and the damp patch on the front of her matching pretty pink lace bra and panties, somehow empowered her. The bulge in Peter's trousers showed that he was every bit as excited as she was. He wanted her and that made everything all right.

She became calmer and she felt her breathing grow less strained as she felt a little of the tension ease from her neck and shoulders. She began to feel comfortable, yet still excited, as she waited for his next instruction.

"How are you feeling?" Peter sat back, his thumb stroking his trousers, lightly just beyond the end of his penis.

"I feel fine, Sir." His words reassured her and she straightened her back.

"Good," Peter paused, "are you excited?"

The answer to the question was obvious in the wet stain on the front of her panties and the erect peaks of her nipples showing through her bra. He could see how excited she was but she hesitated to voice how excited she was.

"I would like you to tell me how excited you are. I know you find it difficult to verbalize this... But I want you to try."

"Yes Sir," her voice trembled and her face flushed. "I am very excited, Sir." Why should this be so hard to say out loud? She didn't understand why, but it was and she felt a little embarrassed to say it.

"Good girl. I am very pleased with you. "Pleased with her? Did he think of her as a pet? She should have been angry, yet she wasn't. She was quite the opposite. She was proud that he was pleased with her. She was proud of being strong enough to do what he had asked and she replied with a simple, "Thank you, Sir."

Peter continued to stroke his leg, his thumb now catching the tip of his member on each stroke. "Your bra now, please." The tone in his voice had not altered; he was totally calm, totally in control.

She shrugged one of the shoulder straps down and unclasped the hooks and her soft firm breasts swung free.

The cool air caressed her firm orbs and erect nipples. She felt calm and relaxed, showing Peter her charms. Her eyes flicked over her pale breasts crowned with erect pink gumdrop nipples. His smiling face and hard cock told her all she needed to know. She wanted this man.

The instruction to remove her last garment could not be far away yet it seemed an age before he said, "And now Evelyn, your panties please." She had been expecting that, and shimmied out of the lacy material. What she hadn't expected was his next request. "Would you be so kind as to hand them to me?" Again, the power of this simple request hit her and she handed him the damp swatch of fabric.

Naked and vulnerable now, she looked down at her own body, her erect nipples and damp pubic hair, and the moistness on her thigh. She felt so exposed that she wanted to hide. Her natural instincts made her attempt to cover her body with her hands.

Peter with an almost inaudible "No" stopped her. "You have nothing to worry about you have a lovely body. Let me feast my eyes upon it."

She stood still as she watched him looking at her, then she saw him switch his attention to her panties. As he fingered the cloth, she could almost feel his hands on her. She watched him scrutinize this most intimate piece of clothing. She felt a little embarrassed as he lifted the cloth to his nose and inhaled her scent. She hoped she smelled sweet. His facial expression reassured her. He obviously liked her musk.

Peter's attention moved from her to her panties and back again. When he looked at her she could see he looked at her naked body approvingly. Peter had a look in his eye that said he could and would devour her and she liked that.

"You have never given yourself to a man this way before," he held her panties to his face and inhaled again, "and it troubles you a little…yet it excites you too?" Peter's voice was calm as if he was talking about the weather.

"Yes Sir… very much," her voice was trembling and

husky. She could not disguise the fact she wanted him. As she stood, her legs parted a little and she gave a little sigh as a cool wisp of air whispered across her labia. She was hungry.

Peter looked directly into her eyes. "I want you." He stood and moved to her.

Evelyn dropped her gaze but Peter lifted her chin. His hand was warm and smooth. He looked her directly in the eyes again, and stroked her cheek.

With her face in his hands Peter whispered, "I want you to give yourself to me. I want you to do it totally. I want you to do it willingly and without reservation. Do you give yourself to me?"

She felt her face melt into his hands, she felt her knees tremble. There and then, she would do *anything* he asked. "Oh, God yes." she gasped. "Yes Sir, whatever you wish of me."

"Without reservation?" Peter stroked her cheek and looked her in the eyes, never breaking eye contact.

Evelyn blurted out, "Yes Sir. I will do anything." Her words left her lips without the full implication of what *anything* could mean. There was nothing this man could ask her to do that she would not do for him. She was his. Her body shook.

"Thank you. I would like you to turn around for me."

Slowly she turned for him and though she could not see his face, the small grunts he gave, reassured her that he appreciated her back view every bit as much as he had the front.

"Truly exquisite," whispered Peter. His words were reverent, as if describing a work of art.

Peter held her from behind and whispered in her ear. "You are beautiful, truly beautiful. I wish to prepare you, *to make you even more perfect*. Please show me the way to your bathroom."

His words reassured her. It was as if her every nerve was attuned and alert. Evelyn caught the smell of his subtle citrus aftershave, as she led him to the bathroom. She felt the carpet beneath her naked toes, as she crossed the living room. She felt the blood pounding in her veins. A million questions went through her mind. Whatever would this preparation entail? Were they to shower? Was he to wash her? She knew better than to ask, yet her mind and heart raced.

They walked through her bedroom to get to the bathroom. She was proud of her bedroom's décor. It had an air of elegance, as did her bathroom. In the bathroom, she looked around trying to imagine what Peter would think. It was a large opulent room with cool marble tiled floor and walls, sophisticated antique mirrors, and art deco light fittings. Matching pink towels and floor mats and gold plated fittings crowned the appearance. She could see Peter looking around and hoped he was impressed.

He nodded approvingly and turned her to face him. "Very nice, I like it." He kept eye contact with her and continued, "Do you have a new razor?" Peter's voice was still calm.

Evelyn did not know why she trusted him, but she did, yet the request for a razor presented a new level of trust. Never had she had such an experience. Every fibre in her being, said this is not how couples made out, she should resist, yet in the same breath it felt so right to submit to this man's will. She felt like she was on a rollercoaster ride, nervous, yet at the same time excited beyond words.

Evelyn handed the razor to Peter.

He smiled reassuringly, "You don't need to look so worried." He kissed her on her lips, "I am not going to hurt you." He held her by the waist and kissed her tenderly again.

She melted into his kiss. She felt relieved at the normality of this one simple natural act.

It was Peter that broke the kiss. He looked deeply into her eyes and said, "You really are a very special lady." She bubbled over with emotions. Tears welled in her eyes. All she wanted right then was to be with Peter, to do anything he wanted her to do, regardless of what it might be. Anything!

With a last kiss, Peter knelt before her. He had lathered a bar of scented soap and was massaging the foam into her pubis. She felt his hands, strong yet gentle, pressing on her delicate flesh. She felt cherished and pampered. She exulted in her desire. He was her Master. Her body was his to do with as he wanted and it was as she accepted that her body was in Peter's control that he began to shave off her already closely trimmed pubic hair.

She looked down intently, relaxed yet fascinated as she watched his nimble fingers part her petals, opening her to the blade. His hands were steady and deftly every hair was removed, as he shaved her smooth.

Peter moved back to admire his work and smiled. "I much prefer your treasure in the open rather than hiding in the shadows. I wish you to keep yourself smooth from now on."

"Yes Sir."

She stood looking down helplessly, as Peter leaned forward and kissed her clit, holding her morsel between his lips. Holding her hips, he feasted with lips and tongue, teasing her pearl from the shell. The feeling was so intense, the contact so immediate she could do nothing but cum under his ministrations. She screamed and convulsed, as the spasms tore through her. Every nerve ending was alive. The release so complete, she would have collapsed if he had not been holding her. She felt spent, totally drained and totally relaxed. Peter swept her up in his arms and carried her to the adjoining bedroom. He let Evelyn rest as he removed his own clothes. As his speech, he did not hurry to remove his clothes. He was precise, and after removing each item, it was folded and put neatly on the back of a bedroom chair. Evelyn was captivated by this tall handsome man, so measured in his actions. She watched him strip and all the time he looked at her.

He thumbed down his last garment and his erect penis

sprang out. Evelyn observed that he was a full seven inches long and was more than average in girth. She also noticed immediately that although he had a downy covering of hair on his chest, his groin was shaved smooth. She could not take her eyes of his magnificent erect phallus. She wondered what it would feel like inside her, wondered at the taste of his semen.

Peter crossed to her. "I think you are recovered enough," he smiled, as he looked down at her.

"May I ask a question, Sir?" her eyes were fixed to his firm body.

"Of course."

"I thought I was to serve you?" her eyes were warm and there was a glow still on her cheeks.

"You will serve me, and you will serve me all the better now that your lust has been sated." His hand idly toyed with his erect penis. "You were burning with lust my pet. Now you will serve me with your full attention on my needs." He walked to where she sat on the edge of the bed. "And you will start by paying homage to my cock." He offered the head to her lips and she opened to receive him.

Peter was large but not uncomfortably so. Evelyn ran the tip of her tongue over his satin dome. She licked and sucked his member taking it, little by little, deeper into her mouth. She wanted to give Peter as much pleasure as he had given her; she wanted to give him more. She understood then, the logic of Peter's earlier action. Her head rose and sunk on his shaft. She made her lips tight for him covering her teeth, so as not to nip him.

Up to this point, Peter had let her set the pace, but now she felt his needs taking over. She felt his big firm hands cradling the back of her head and felt him began to rock back and forth. It was not unpleasant and she held her mouth still as he fucked her. She heard him moan as he took his pleasure. His rhythm and depth of stroke increased. She could feel the thrust of his length travel within her mouth, suddenly the strokes changed to short sharp thrusts and she knew he was drawing close. One deep thrust and he remained still. Evelyn could feel him pulse, as she received his liquid gift.

They cuddled for a while naked on the bed, in the spoons position, his cock between the cheeks of her bottom, his arms wrapped around her. She felt warm, safe and loved. As they drifted off to sleep, Evelyn reviewed the evening's events.

She had agreed without reservation, she had surprised herself with this. Normally she was assertive, but she felt great comfort in submitting to Peter. It felt like she had discovered her true nature in the submission, and she felt stronger knowing that Peter was there. This was their first time together as lovers and yet she felt like she had known him forever, felt like she would do anything for him. She felt like she was his and only his. In an instant, she thought of her previous lovers and realized no one had ever made her feel this way. She knew at that point, that Peter was the one for her.

Over the coming months, Evelyn gave more and more of herself to Peter. His control was like a drug; the more she had the more she wanted. Peter provided the focus to her daily life. Even when they were parted, it was like he was with her in spirit. She loved the way that he would choose her clothing for the day. He would decide what they would eat. Some people would find it troubling or oppressive to have someone decide. Evelyn found her day a brighter place knowing that she served Peter. She found a profound sense of comfort and shelter in Peter's love.

The internet showed a world of those who lead and those who follow, gladly and willingly. People in the know called it *the scene* and it was a world filled with dominants and submissives.

She had been terrified, the first time Peter took her to a dominance and submission club, but once there she saw it as just a place where like-minded people came to hang out.

Evelyn spent more time in the company of other submissives. Listening to their stories made her feel more at home with this new lifestyle that she heard them refer to as *the scene*. The easy matter-of-fact way they described their own service made her more comfortable with this way of life than she had ever been in the vanilla world.

As her experience and confidence grew, she found her love for Peter growing. She found herself stopping during the course of the day thinking of what he might be up to. Her life seemed focused around his wants and needs. She began to anticipate things that he might like. As he lay out the clothes he wished her to wear, she made sure he was well turned out, taking a delight in polishing his shoes, even ironing shirts was no longer a chore, for it was for her Master. Listening to the other subs, she found new ways to verbalize their relationship and she learned to speak of their love. She heard other subs call their Doms *Master*, and she liked the term. To her ears, it sounded loving and respectful and she wanted to please her master so much. She would never forget the way Peter's face lit up the first time she had called him *Master*. She loved the way it sounded and it was a title she called him gladly. She could not conceive of her life without her Master in complete control. This was no abusive slave relationship. The power he had she gave him freely.

They shared, what they came to refer to as training sessions, where Peter would introduce her to new things like nipple clamps and toys and plugs. Together they would sit and trawl the internet and Peter would explain the significance of the lifestyle in their daily lives. Each new experience brought them closer together physically and spiritually.

It took a year with the help of books, videos, and the internet, for Peter to help her come to grips with the complexity of the scene. They talked passionately for hours long into the night. Evelyn loved the way he taught her. It was done with love and affection. Each session was slow and unhurried. It was consensual, he had always insisted on that.

She remembered a time when he wished her to go though the next stage and meet other Doms and subs in the flesh. She was terrified.

He had spent hours preparing her, dressing her to the nines, in stockings and a tight leather corset. Yet, despite all the preparations, he had asked her if she wanted to go in. It was her free choice. And she loved him for that.

It was with that love, she gathered her courage and went into the gathering, that she later found out they call a *munch*. She and Peter became regulars for a while and she observed close hand all manner of things that were new to her, the art of Japanese bondage, suspension, piercing, scarification, all manner of different forms of corporal punishment and secretly she wished it were she that felt the taste of the whip and crop.

Every aspect of her life Peter made his masterly presence felt. Evelyn remembered the day a bouquet of roses had been delivered to her private office. The delivery boy entered and presented her the bouquet of a dozen roses. Her heart had leapt for joy, a present from her master, a token of his love for her. She sniffed the rose. The fragrance matched its beauty. She turned her attention to the card and smiled when she read; *For you my darling, you serve me so beautifully well, now as a token of your service to me, I wish you to remove your panties and give them to the delivery boy.* Without a doubt, the boy had read the card, if the smirk on his face was anything to go by. How could she do anything but comply? As embarrassed as she was and with as much dignity as she could muster, she wiggled out of her panties and handed them to the young man. He thanked her and left and she was left to think about it for the rest of her working day.

These games were more than a little embarrassing, yet they were a fun part of their relationship and she loved them. She loved the comfort she found in his control and the shelter within his power. The more he asked of her, the more she wanted to give. Peter was experienced in this way of life, although only two years older, at thirty-five he had the self-confidence to know what he wanted. Evelyn felt secure; it was as if she had waited her life for him.

After the visits to the *munches*, Peter introduced her to the kaleidoscope of things she has seen demonstrated in the club. These would challenge her perceptions of what was right and wrong in relationships. At this time, there were so many firsts, the night she had submitted to bondage, her first spanking, the bite of nipple clamps, and the myriad of toys, whips and floggers, all for their mutual pleasure. Evelyn learned not to tease Peter, as that would surely not work out as she had planned.

Occasionally she had tried to get the upper hand but try as she might she never did. She remembered teasing him one day, keeping him in a state of excitement, and then informing him that sadly it was the wrong time of the month. It had been her way of trying to turn the tables on her Master, but Peter did not flinch. He took a coin from his pocket and flipped it. "Now we will see. Heads or Tails" and with the tails side of the coin showing, another first, was added to her list. Sodomy. It was new to her, but she trusted her Master completely and submitted freely to this new act.

Day by day, week by week and as month followed month, Peter took Evelyn to her very limits, and she went there willingly. She was his and wanted nothing else.

Over dinner one night Peter had said, "My pet, this is my nature, and I believe this is in your nature too, although as people we are free and equal, our nature leads us to a different reality. I believe you feel the same and instinctively know what I am saying. It is my belief you wish to serve me, as much as I wish you to serve."

Peter opened a small black velvet box. Inside was a short gold chain, in the middle of which was a small amulet inscribed with an ornately inscribed letter *P*. "my pet, this is for you, I would like to marry you, but it is fair for you to know, truly know, my heart's desire. With this chain, you will serve me, as I will cherish, protect, and nurture you. In the marriage service, they use the words love, honor and obey. In the world, I want us to live in; I want those words to be very literal. I wish you to honor and obey me, and with that, I pledge myself only to you. Will you take this chain? Will you serve me and only me, will you marry me?"

Then as now, a tear trickled down her cheek and she said aloud, as she had done then, "I will." Plain and simple, yet profound. She wanted nothing more. With his proposal and her acceptance, her life was complete.

There seemed no end to this golden time. Yet, like all golden times, it had to end and when it did, it crushed her.

The thought buzzed through her mind and a tear rolled down her cheek. A golden time, but that had been four years ago. And here she was now, driving through the night.

The lights cut through the night, lighting trees and flickering across the houses, which were scattered sparsely throughout this part of the countryside. The hotel had been built in the middle of nowhere and the remoteness had been the reason they had picked it for their honeymoon, all those years ago.

She knew she was drawing close to her destination, although time had taken it toll on the landscape. The road lacked the quaintness it once had and the small shrines situated on sharp bends, gave testimony to how much more dangerous the roads had become over the years. There was the old mailbox once a bright red, now faded to a drab grey. An old oak tree who's once majestic lower branches, were now loped off. There were more than a dozen markers she used to navigate this journey and though the landmarks were older and shabbier, they were still unmistakable. She had never been great at navigation, especially out of town but although remote, she had never had any difficulty finding *Woodside Manor*.

There was a small crest to a hill before the approach to the Manor. Evelyn caught her breath as the lights played across the building, lighting the two majestic towers that flanked either side of the castellated top of the main building.

Woodside manor had once been an exclusive country club, owned by an oil tycoon. No expense had been spared on its original construction. It had enjoyed a second life as a luxury hotel, but successive owners, had let it fall into disrepair.

Evelyn's sleek, burgundy-colored Jaguar turned off the main road and up the long, winding, tree lined driveway, which led to the hotel. As she approached, her lights swung across the faded façade that had once been a gleaming white. There was a fountain in the middle of a large doughnut shaped parking area. It was once lit and the jets of water then had been bathed in colored light. Now it was dark and the water danced no more. The water was green and stagnant and the ornamental statue in the centre of the pond was covered with a thick moss concealing that it had once been an attractive lady holding a Greek urn.

From the first time she had visited the manor she had loved the place. The opulence of the frontage had always reminded her of the set in the film *Gone with the Wind*. The building seemed steeped in southern colonial elegance. She felt a little saddened to see this grand building, now so down at heel. The gardens too, what she could see of them, were a faded reminder of what had once been.

Woodside Manor was no longer the prestigious venue for millionaires and playboys; it had faded, as all things fade in time.

The tires crunched to a halt and Evelyn sat in the car, with the engine still running. She touched the amulet at her throat. The chain was short enough to draw comment. A close friend had once said that the medallion on such a short collar resembles a dog's collar. The comment had made Evelyn smile and she drew her own comparison with the ownership of her as the beloved pet. Of course, a vanilla world could not see what it was, it simply made them curious. She fingered the decorative rose gold *P* and she thought of her service and what the collar represented.

She turned the key and the car's quiet hum fell silent. Evelyn sat still in the car, aware of the gifts she wore in honor of Peter. Conflict swirled in her mind. In the dark, her fingers fiddled with the car door latch. It clicked and swung open, but as she left the car, she went cold, as she thought of her husband James. Another wave of guilt tore through her. After all James had done for her, how could she do this to him? How could she betray him like this? Yet her passion for her Master was strong.

Her mind turned over the argument; she felt a strong commitment to both men. In a way, she had betrayed Peter in marrying James. Peter had been her Master for many years before she had known James. Her loyalties ran deep with both men. She loved them both. She would do anything for James, except this one thing, this one day of the year she must honor the vows she had made to her Master. How she wanted Peter. This was beyond animal lust, though in truth she felt that too, this was a bond. She had a commitment to Peter that no mortal could break. She knew no matter what, Peter loved her as deeply as she loved him.

She sat in the car gathering her thoughts for a brief moment, pondering her next move, although the choice had already been made. The choice had been made the day she said, *"I do"* to Peter.

The time of doubt was over. There was a way of getting out of the Jaguar that was more graceful than others. She had become quite expert at doing it. Keeping her knees together, she swung her legs around so she still sat on the seat, but now with her feet on the graveled car park. Then she stood. The alternative method of getting out of a low sports car, especially wearing a short skirt, was far too revealing.

Locking the car, she took the opportunity to take a closer

look around the car park. Evelyn caught her breath, as she saw Peter's black sports car, with an ominous dent in the front driver's side wing. She walked over to the car and felt the contours of the indentation. She realized, as she ran her hand along the distorted shape of the depression, that the sleek paintwork had not even been broken. Her feelings turned to warmth, as she smiled, thinking back to that happy day when Peter first showed her the car. It was gleaming new, with just the showroom miles on the clock. He was like a small boy with a new toy, eager to show the trivial gadgets that please men so much in their toys. With a last stroke of the paintwork, she turned to the hotel.

Her black stiletto heels crunched, as she crossed the fine pea shingle to the still impressive, yet faded, front door. The closer Evelyn got to him, the more she realized how much she still needed him. She wanted him more now than ever. She moistened at the thought of him using her body. She was so ready; she wondered how he would have her. Would his mood today be rough or smooth?

In her minds eye, she pictured herself tied, naked and helpless. She pictured his strong hands running over her body. She thought of the pinch of clamps on her tender parts, the smack of paddle, the bee sting of riding crop. A year had been a long time since she had felt Master's firm discipline and she longed to succumb to his will.

She wondered if Peter's features had changed over the last year. Would he look different? Any older? She had scrutinized her facial lines while she was preparing herself for this visit. Her bathroom at home had a shelf dedicated to creams and lotions, making claims to rejuvenate the skin, yet the lines crept in. Were it not for her weekly visit to the hairdresser, she knew that grey whips would streak her hair. But she did not do grey.

Would Peter's hair have aged? He would never be vain enough to use a color. Would his nice physique sport a curve of tummy as age took its toll? All the time she daydreamed, thinking of the changes she might see, she hoped that this evening, would be exactly as if it had been when they lived as man and wife. A pang of desire drove her on.

She wanted Peter alone in the privacy of their bedroom. She wanted to submit to her Master in whatever way he wanted her. Deep down, she never wanted this evening to end.

Once in the lobby the man at the reception desk didn't look up from the sports section in his newspaper, as she crossed the threadbare carpet on the way to the elevator. The interior was faded yet still clues to its former splendor were there. The art deco light fittings, antique mirrors, ornate plasterwork ceilings, and once plush couches at the edges of the large foyer all spoke of a more opulent time yet there was a grubby feel now. Unkempt plants sat on scarred wood tables and a stale musty smell filled the air.

Evelyn entered the elevator and selected the fourth floor. She found herself trembling slightly, as she approached the door to their room. Butterflies danced in her stomach. It had been a whole year since she had last seen Peter.

A flood of emotions hit her and she stayed motionless for a moment. In one breath, she knew that Peter meant everything to her, yet the trembled like a sophomore on her first date.

A shiver passed over Evelyn and suddenly she went as cold as the grave. Peter, James, her life, her loves, her heart, like a near death experience, she saw herself from above. Her life flashed before her eyes. The conflicts and emotions whirled around her head and in one instant there was a part of her that just wanted to run, run back to the arms of James. She was torn between the safety and security of home and the call of her Master.

It had been four years since she had served him full time, yet the power of his voice rang loud and clear in her ears. How she wanted the touch of his hand. She needed Peter. All the time there was Peter, always Peter and she knew as surely as night followed day that she would take these last few steps and knock on the door.

It was the same room where they had made love for more years than she could recall. The same room where she had spent her honeymoon, the room where her lover waited silently for her now.

Her eyes lingered on the tarnished brass numbers 422. There on the door below the number was their sign, a rose, now slightly wilted, yet nevertheless a symbol of their love. A fingertip stroked a slightly wilting petal and with a deep breath and a trembling hand Evelyn's knuckle lightly rapped on the door. With a sigh, her full breasts swelled against her starched linen blouse and suddenly she was fully aware of herself again, aware of the very personal way Peter has asked her to dress for his pleasure. She felt the intimacy and closeness of the chain, as she waited for a response. The metal stroked tender flesh. She could sense, just how wet she was in anticipation of this meeting. A nervous hand fiddled with the hem of her skirt.

For what seemed like an age, she waited outside the door, then the solid click of the lock and there stood Peter, crisp white shirt, and his charcoal business suit. Gold cufflinks and tiepin and the shine on his shoes. He was just the same as he ever was, he had not changed, not one wrinkle, not one additional grey hair. Tears welled up in her eyes as the love for her master overwhelmed her She caught her breath and stifled a sob, as she saw the fire red tie with the tiny white dots she had bought him so many years ago. She looked him full in the face. Yes, he was just the same. The broad, open smile and the glint in his eye, took her back to the electronics trade show where they had met, all those years ago.

She had always loved his enthusiasm, no matter what he did, he always did it keenly. How she loved him. Evelyn stepped to her Master and melted into his waiting arms as if she had never been parted from him.

She felt Peter give the door a gentle push, with a solid

click, the door closed, and they were alone.

Their embrace lasted an age, and even then only broke reluctantly.

It was Peter who stepped back, to admire his beautiful lady. She had dressed according to his requests and he appreciated her attention to detail. Her full creamy breasts thrust against her crisp white blouse, her black skirt hugged her rounded hips. His gaze traveled down to her gorgeous stockinged legs and stylish Italian high heels and then back up where the whole image was crowned by the broad gold chain that hung high around her neck, resembling a collar. Affixed to the chain was an amulet, a yellow gold disk with his initial *P* inlaid in rose gold. On the flipside the maker's mark, which as a smaller yet no less impressive *Z*. The amulet matched the pendent that hung around his own neck, only the inscription on the front was an elaborate *E*.

www.blackvelvetseductions.com

Available Now
From Black Velvet Seductions
Forbidden Experiences

The Crimson Z
By: Robert Cloud
Lee Rush
Richard Savage
Abby Blythe
Kara Elsberry

Zachariah was a true craftsman. It was the passion to reach true perfection that drove him to work long after he should have retired. His work imbued him with a life that few could imagine. With the aid of the spirit of his long dead wife each piece of jewelry that was commissioned not only restored years to Zachariah's life but imbedded each piece with a special magic..

Several masterpieces of jewelry, each bearing the maker's mark of the crimson Z... Five stories of romance, each written by a different Black Velvet Seductions' author... All told from the lips of an old jeweler who is falling in love with a girl way too young for him.

Will the jewelry in each of the stories bring the wearer love or will it be a curse releasing unthinkable evil on unsuspecting lovers?

Available Now in
Paperback and ebook

www.blackvelvetseductions.com

Available Now
From Black Velvet Seductions
Forbidden Experiences

The Stir of Echo
By: Susan Gabriel

A gifted, but untrained clairaudient with a secret desire to be dominated is about to find out the truth behind the old adage, "Be careful what you wish for, because you just might get it."

Echo Sullivan has all but given up on herself, her gift, and on men, until she meets her charming new neighbor, Flynn. An invitation to his Halloween Fantasy Ball sends her on a course of discovery, and sexual awakening with life-altering choices.

Flynn's rakish good looks, sharp wit, and smooth Irish brogue appear to be just what the doctor ordered. He possesses an unsettling ability to recognize, and illuminate Echo's deepest desires; to stir them up and bring them bubbling to the surface. But Flynn harbors a strange and extraordinary secret.

What would you say if someone offered you the world…but asked for your soul?

Available Now in
Paperback and ebook

www.blackvelvetseductions.com

Available Now
From Black Velvet Seductions
Forbidden Experiences

Toy's Story
Acquisition of a Sex Toy
Book #1 Master's Circle
By: Robert Cloud

David and Doreen used the Internet to start a romance that centered on her fantasy to kneel at his feet as a slave. When her real life interfered with her Internet fantasy life she left the fantasy behind.

But when the fantasy is who you are it becomes overpowering. Doreen could not stop wishing for the fantasy that was out of reach.

When she could no longer deny the powerful fantasy she begged David, her online Master to rescue her from her vanilla life. He complied, fulfilling her wishes in a way that she had not dared to consider even in her most wild and erotic fantasies.

"Compelling and emotional, Robert Cloud has written a story that will dig into the depths of the emotions and settle deep into the heart. No punches are pulled in this gritty, tough story and the characters are bared on each and every level of existence." —Valerie a reviewer at Love Romances

Available Now in
Paperback and ebook

www.blackvelvetseductions.com

Available Now
From Black Velvet Seductions
Forbidden Experiences

Bound by Fate
By Lee Rush

Sometimes love by itself is not enough.

James and Annie are mature adults who meet on line and discover a powerful attraction that grows stronger as they explore their mutual interest in BDSM. When they meet in person the attraction they felt online grows into full fledged love and their online exploration of the master and slave lifestyle spills into reality. But even the bond of love they have built isn't enough to sustain their relationship in the face of obstacles which neither can alter.

After their relationship is torn apart, their love nearly destroyed, fate steps in and allows them another chance. "Bound by Fate" is the story of two people who are given a second chance to make their dreams come true.

Available Now in
Paperback and ebook

Black Velvet Seductions
1350-C W Southport Rd, Box 249
Indianapolis, IN 46217

www.blackvelvetseductions.com